THE
OTHER SIDE
OF
THE WALL

ALSO BY AMY EPHRON

The Castle in the Mist
Carnival Magic

THE
OTHER SIDE
OF
THE WALL

AMY EPHRON

PHILOMEL BOOKS

PHILOMEL BOOKS
An imprint of Penguin Random House LLC, New York

First published in the United States of America by Philomel Books,
an imprint of Penguin Random House LLC, 2019.

Visit us online at penguinrandomhouse.com

LIBRARY OF CONGRESS CATALOGING-IN-PUBLICATION DATA
Names: Ephron, Amy, author.
Title: The other side of the wall / Amy Ephron.
Description: New York : Philomel Books, [2019] | Companion to: Castle
in the mist and Carnival magic. | Summary: "Tess and Max encounter a new
adventure through time, this time in London at Christmas"—Provided by
publisher. | Identifiers: LCCN 2018056331| ISBN 9781984813275 (hardcover)
| ISBN 9781984813282 (e-book) | Subjects: | CYAC: Spirit possession—Fiction. |
Brothers and sisters—Fiction. | Christmas—Fiction. | London (England)—Fiction. |
England—Fiction. | Classification: LCC PZ7.1.E62 Oth 2019 |
DDC [Fic] —dc23 LC record available at https://lccn.loc.gov/2018056331

Printed in Canada
ISBN 9781984813275
1 3 5 7 9 10 8 6 4 2

Edited by Jill Santopolo. Design by Jennifer Chung.
Text set in 12.25-point Winchester New ITC Std.

For Chloe, Roman,
& the man in the bowler hat

THE
SANBORN
HOUSE

CONTENTS

maybe it's the wind

Did you see that?"

"See what?" Max replied.

"That . . . that shadow that went past the window," said Tess, "out in the garden." *It was more than a shadow, a shape that had streaked by the window.* She couldn't explain what it was.

Tess and Max were sharing a suite at a small, somewhat trendy hotel in London called **THE SANBORN HOUSE**.

They had gone to meet their mom and dad and Aunt Evie for Christmas break, although their parents hadn't arrived yet.

Tess would be sleeping in the bedroom. Max had a rollaway cot in the living room. At the moment, Tess was sitting on the antique carpet on the floor of the living room and Max was lying on his freshly made cot. They had checked in at the desk with Aunt Evie, found their hotel room, and obediently unpacked their suitcases.

They were both a little tired from the trip to London. Tess was staring vacantly out the window to the garden. Except she'd noticed something. Or at least she thought she had. It looked like a shape that had streaked quickly past the window—not an animal, something else, shadowy, which had sneaked past, not blown by the wind.

"I didn't see anything," said Max immediately, definitively, even though he was sitting up as if he had.

"But," he added, "there could be a number of explanations for it." There was a bit of an edge to his voice, as if he was irritated at Tess. And Tess noticed she hadn't told him, at all, what she'd seen and nonetheless he was rationalizing it for her. Ever logical, he explained, "For instance, a cloud passed across the sun, causing a shadow."

"We're in London, there isn't any sun," said Tess, not meaning to be funny.

Max hesitated, and then suggested gruffly, as if he wished this conversation would be over, "A large truck passed by in the alley then and altered the light."

"I don't think there is an alley," said Tess. "It looks like there's just a garden that separates our hotel from the back of the house on the street behind us. I bet the garden's pretty in the spring," she added.

"It's pretty now," said Max.

It was unusually cold, and the branches of the trees were gilded with ice and an occasional dangling icicle that oddly reflected what little light there was into colored patterns, the way a glass prism would.

"You're right," said Tess. "It is pretty. And the icicles are natural holiday tree decorations. I bet Mom would like them. And see those red berries dotting that bush? I wonder what kind of berry bush it is."

Max almost snapped at her, "Can we look it up before we test one? Or at least ask someone what it is?"

"Promise," said Tess who started laughing for a second until she realized Max hadn't meant *that* to be funny. She hesitated. "You didn't see anything? Really?!" she asked again. "But, what I saw was, umm"—she didn't really want to use the word, but she couldn't help it—"ghostly."

The wind was blowing, as if in punctuation, a cold and scary wind, rattling the windows.

"Okay, shadowy, then," said Tess modifying her thought so as not to frighten Max unnecessarily. "You didn't see it?" she repeated.

But before Max could answer, Aunt Evie burst in to their hotel room without knocking. "Oh my," she said, "put on your hat and grab your mittens."

She probably meant, put on your mittens and grab your hat, but neither one of them corrected her.

"I think it's going to snow," Aunt Evie said. "It never snows in London. Well, hardly ever. And when it does," she said, "it's a very magical time to go out."

Aunt Evie was wearing a gray and white scarf tied around her neck and tucked stylishly into her gray wool coat.

Max grabbed his hoodie. Aunt Evie shook her head. "Don't you have something warmer?" she asked, and also nodded to his sneakers and suggested, "Boots?"

Both Tess and Max had lots of warm clothes as they'd been sent back to school in Switzerland in September. Their mom and dad had rented out their apartment in New York City and their mother had moved to Germany to be with their dad who was stationed there, now, in Berlin as the head of the International News Desk.

Tess didn't really understand why they couldn't go to the American School in Berlin. But it seemed like their parents needed a little time to try to sort things out.

Tess hated the sound of that. "Sort things out." She and Max had heard them have a fight one night during dinner, which was very unusual. It was the night their dad had said "family conference" and told them and their mom that he'd accepted the job in Berlin. Tess understood why her mom could get mad about her dad taking the job in Berlin, but she also understood why he took it. It was an amazing opportunity. But they started to have a fight. Tess and Max excused themselves from the dinner table. Shortly thereafter, their mom had left and closed the door to the apartment so loudly the walls seemed to shake, and she didn't come back for at least four hours.

After that, their parents had been civil with each other but somewhat distant, or at least Tess thought that was the case. Not as affectionate as they had always been.

Their dad left for Berlin. And after some persuasion, which involved flowers arriving regularly, sometimes even twice a week, roses, peonies, lilies, orchids, and late night whispered conversations that Tess and Max only caught a word or two of, their mom decided to join him in Berlin in September.

Tess and Max didn't push their parents on the decision to send them back to boarding school in Switzerland. Although it did seem to Tess that their mom would spend a fair amount of time alone in Germany, as their dad was also reporting on camera from all points abroad, including Russia and the Middle East.

Their father had become quite well-known. It wasn't unusual for someone to ask one of them if they were related to Martin Barnes, the TV news guy. And Tess or Max would say, "Yes," very proudly, "he's my dad."

Tess had been told by a friend's mother that seeing Tess's father on television made her feel a bit more secure, especially since there was so much uncertainty in the world. "There's something about your dad that makes me feel calmer," she said.

Tess *was* proud to hear this and didn't add her own feeling, which was sometimes it made her anxious, especially when he was reporting from a country that was experiencing "unrest." That's what they called it—the preferred expression around their house "unrest"—which could mean a flood or a war-zone.

Tess smiled and told the woman she was pretty proud of her dad, too.

Tess did think both her dad and mom would be excited about the unusual possibility of a snowstorm in London, even if it was only an hour or two long.

Tess buttoned her coat and pulled her collar up and put her mittens on, and as she did, she swore she saw something out the window again, but she didn't say anything. She didn't want Aunt Evie and Max to think she might be imagining things again.

She was quite certain she'd seen it though. *A strange shadow and a shape.* It was probably just a snow flurry.

snowflakes falling

Max shut the hotel room door after them, carefully locking it with a gold key on a silver chain attached to a small wooden plaque that said GARDEN ROOM just in case they forgot what room they were in. The key itself was curious. It had a glass dome on the top, almost like a miniature crystal doorknob, with a spray of orange in the middle, as if it really was blown glass.

Tess put her hand out for the key, but Max shook his

head. He knew enough about Tess and keys in England to decide to keep this one himself. He put it in his fleece jacket pocket, which conveniently had a zipper, which he closed.

They ran through the lobby, as Aunt Evie was walking so quickly it was hard to keep up. Tess practically bumped into an elegant Englishman wearing a bowler hat and a well-fitting pinstripe suit who was accompanied by a small white terrier on a leash who Tess also almost tripped over.

"Sorry," said Tess, first to the dog and then to the gentleman.

"No harm done, was there, Princess?" he said to the dog, who seemed almost to nod at him. "No harm done at all," the gentleman replied.

The terrier nodded happily, but somewhat attitudinally, if a dog can have attitude, and waved her tail, not quite a wag, just a simple wave. Tess noticed there was a pink satin bow tied festively into a tiny bunch of hair on top of the terrier's head, like a ponytail that stuck straight up.

The dog's eyes were fixed on Tess and were remarkably intelligent and dark brown, almost the color of hazelnuts. For a moment, the dog, whose name really was "Princess," sidled up to Tess and brushed her body against Tess's right leg.

"No harm done, at all, Missy," the gentleman insisted. "I think she likes you." Tess noticed that the gentleman called her "Missy" which reminded her of what someone else had called her last summer, but sometimes people did that in England. Called people, "Missy," almost as if it was a term of endearment or respect.

Tess leaned down and patted the top of Princess's head, being careful not to disturb the bow, smiled politely at the gentleman, and ran off to try to catch Max and Aunt Evie, who were halfway out the front door of the hotel. She joined them out on the sidewalk where the wind was blowing umbrellas upside down and a light snow was falling steadily.

The doorman was in the street blowing his whistle, but no one was stopping, and it looked as if there were two couples and one family of five ahead of them. The wind was practically wailing, and the snow was falling rapidly, almost at an angle, but the snowflakes were so tiny, they were as soft as cotton powder puffs floating in the air. Tess thought it was oddly refreshing, and she imagined sparkles when the snowflakes landed daintily on her cheeks. She looked over at Aunt Evie and her cheeks were sparkly, too.

Aunt Evie was tapping her foot impatiently. Aunt Evie didn't like it when the trains didn't run smoothly.

That was an expression their mom sometimes used. It meant that everything was delayed, which in this case was actually true, as Aunt Evie had informed them, when she picked them up at Heathrow Airport, that their parents' plane from Berlin had been delayed due to stormy weather—so delayed, they hadn't even waited at the airport since *nothing* was taking off or landing. They had told Aunt Evie they would try to get another plane tomorrow. Tess and Max didn't mind that much although they were looking forward to seeing their parents. It was always lovely to spend time with Aunt Evie.

Aunt Evie wasn't in the mood to wait. She saw an old-fashioned carriage parked at the curb with a white horse whose well-brushed mane also seemed to sparkle when the snowflakes landed on it.

Aunt Evie smiled impishly at Tess and Max and took both their hands. "Be careful. It's slippery," she said as she walked quickly with them to the corner.

The carriage driver just stared straight ahead.

"Are you hired, Sir?" Aunt Evie asked, tipping her big hat with the flowers slightly to the side as if she was enticing him to look at her.

The driver turned to look at Aunt Evie and at Tess and Max. "Of course, I am," he said slyly, "I've been waiting for you for half an hour."

"You don't mean us?" said Aunt Evie.

"Of course, I do," he answered immediately. "You must be Aunt Evie. And you I suppose must be Tess and Max."

"Well, isn't that a nice surprise," she said. "Your dad must have hired him, don't you think?" she asked Tess and Max.

Tess and Max weren't sure that was true.

But before they could answer, the carriage driver tied the reins and jumped down from his seat. He ceremoniously, with a quiet bow, opened the carriage door, and Aunt Evie stepped delicately and elegantly in and sat in the seat facing backwards, and Max and Tess had no choice except to join her, step in, and sit on the opposite seat facing Aunt Evie.

"Anthony Cortland, M'Lady," the driver said, "at your service." He must have been talking to Aunt Evie but oddly he was looking at Tess.

Tess thought it was a funny coincidence, to be called *Missy* and *M'Lady* in the space of five minutes. Remembering her manners, Tess replied instantly, "Pleased to meet you."

Aunt Evie interrupted her and said, "I'm delighted to meet you, too, Mr. Cortland."

Tess realized it probably was Aunt Evie he had been

speaking to. Except, he *was* wearing a herringbone cap. It reminded Tess of the herringbone cap that Barnaby always wore. Barnaby was the caretaker at their friend William's house (actually it was more like a castle) next door to their aunt's country house in Hampshire. Barnaby had always called her "M'Lady."

With another slight bow just for show, Anthony Cortland shut the door to the carriage and took his place in the driver's seat.

Tess could see him and the back of the white horse through an open window, cut into the front of the cab, she supposed for giving instructions. Mr. Cortland leaned down and said to Tess—she was sure he was speaking to her this time—"Her name's 'Comet,' by the way, just in case you were wondering, and she quite knows her way around London."

Tess watched as Mr. Cortland picked up Comet's reins and, without the use of any kind of riding crop or whip, Mr. Cortland clicked his tongue (or his cheek or something), making a surprisingly loud noise, which Comet responded to immediately. And, as if she was a trained trick pony used to dancing, Comet started to pull them quickly and merrily down the street, which was paved with cobblestones so that every hoof beat was like a rhythmic underpinning to the snow falling lightly all around them.

Tess imagined they were in a snow globe. One that her mother could keep on her desk, and inside it would be a horse and carriage on a cobblestoned street that was lined with gray stone mansions side-by-side. And when you turned it upside down and turned it back again, the snow would fall in tiny petals around the carriage in the glass.

CHAPTER THREE

a visit to the park

Mr. Cortland leaned his head into the window, looked at Aunt Evie and asked, "And which park did *you* want to be going to, M'Lady?"

Max wanted to point out that they hadn't told him they wanted to go to a park, at all. But before he had a chance to, Aunt Evie replied, "Why Hyde Park, naturally. I know it's only a few blocks away, but I saw you at the curb and thought it would be fun to ride in a horse and carriage and I had no idea you were waiting for us . . ."

Mr. Cortland smiled, sat back up, and clicked his tongue again, and Comet made a right turn as if the horse did know exactly where she was going.

Tess was impressed how well Aunt Evie knew London. The way she'd immediately answered, "Why Hyde Park, naturally." Tess knew Evie had lived here with Uncle John. But she was starting to realize Aunt Evie was sophisticated, worldly, self-assured, and as they'd always suspected, quite opinionated.

As they pulled up to the park, there was already snow on the ground. Max jumped out of the carriage, as he saw some kids playing with a large slip of cardboard sliding down a hill and wanted to go join them.

Aunt Evie and Tess followed and watched as he made a friend who let him use the cardboard and Max very happily slid down the hill. Snow was falling all around them. Max's cheeks were rosy and a little sparkly, too. And he was smiling.

He joined Tess and Aunt Evie. He noticed Tess was staring off in the distance. She almost thought she was imagining it.

"You're not imagining that," said Max before Tess could even ask the question.

Off in the distance was the distinct image of a Ferris wheel.

Aunt Evie looked over, as well, and she explained. "There's a winter carnival in Hyde Park," Aunt Evie said. "It was on my list," she added, "but I thought we should wait till your parents get here—it's remarkable to go at night. There's a festival of lights."

Tess and Max weren't quite sure after the experience they had last summer at the carnival that they wanted to find out *how* remarkable it was.

Tess said quickly, "There are so many things to do in London. Why don't we see what Mom and Dad want to do and what you want, Aunt Evie? I know Max wanted to see the changing of the guard at Buckingham Palace. I sort of want to see that, too."

At the same time, Tess couldn't help but feel drawn to the carnival even though she didn't mean to be. She could hear the music in the distance. She wondered if there were rides besides the Ferris wheel and if there was a skating rink with professional ice-skaters dancing in a show. She wondered if there were elves and reindeer. She knew she was too old for elves and reindeer, but she still liked the idea of them. Well, maybe not too old for elves.

"It is sort of magical, isn't it Max, that there's a winter carnival in Hyde Park?"

"Not really," said Max, "it seems logical that there would be a carnival in the park in winter right around Christmas when it snows. And, also a festival of lights is a very normal thing around Christmas. Normal," he repeated just for emphasis.

afternoon tea

The horse and carriage was still parked at the corner outside Hyde Park. Mr. Cortland jumped out the moment he saw them.

"Did you think I wasn't going to wait for you?" he asked.

"Don't know what I thought," said Aunt Evie, "but I'm awfully glad you did."

They bundled cozily into the back seat.

Aunt Evie looked at her iPhone and announced, "Maybe it's a perfect day. I think we'll be back for tea time."

Tess had to admit that so far it had almost been a perfect day.

• • •

The first thing Tess saw when she walked into the dining room at the hotel was a boy, a little older than Tess, maybe fourteen, sitting at a round table covered with a white tablecloth. All the tables were set with elaborate dishes, silver forks and knives, linen napkins, individual teapots, and lovely china tea cups. The boy was having tea by himself. His plate was full and very arranged with a combination of tea sandwiches, three petits fours, and two small scones with whipped cream and raspberries ladled on top of each. And also, in front of him was a full cup of tea, the color of which seemed to indicate he'd added a touch of milk to it, the way Tess liked her tea, too—the English way. Max liked lemon—it was one of the differences between them.

The boy seemed—Tess couldn't quite explain it—lost in thought. Tess couldn't tell if he'd taken even one bite of a sandwich or a nibble of a scone. He was just staring straight ahead.

They sat down at the table just in front of him. Tess tried hard not to turn around and look at him. The waiter was on his way over to take their order. Tess had noticed the boy was elegantly dressed, with a black jacket and a white dress shirt, its cuffs visible, and what seemed to be silver cufflinks in his sleeves.

Max was starving—he was so hungry he wasn't even going to make fun of the tea sandwiches, no comments about cucumber and butter on peculiar triangles of bread that weren't even toasted. He wouldn't complain out loud about Nutella, if that was one of the choices. (Secretly, he was certain that he wasn't the only person who didn't like Nutella.) He would not eat Nutella even if it *was* the only sweet available.

The dining room was half filled. Sitting next to them was an Indian family, two boys and their parents, speaking what Aunt Evie said was Hindi. The mother was wearing a beautiful royal blue sari with stars embroidered on the front. On the other side of their table, two women, who looked a lot like sisters, were also dressed up, wearing silk blouses and very long necklaces. One of the sisters had a large emerald pin on her collar and an even larger emerald on her middle finger. The large emerald was so deep green, it almost looked as if you could fall into it, the way a lake looks in a hidden forest, or if you looked hard enough at it, you might see an image, as if it was related to a crystal ball. Tess stopped herself from imagining that the emerald was sort of a mirror. But she did wonder if she *would* see anything if she looked deeply into the emerald.

"We also have a kids' menu," the waiter said, starting to wheel over another cart. "'Nutella ...'"

"Oh no," Tess interrupted, so Max didn't have to, "we aren't really that fond of Nutella. Aunt Evie says it's 'an acquired taste' and I'm afraid we haven't acquired it yet. My brother hasn't for sure."

Max was embarrassed. He felt his cheeks turning red.

"It also features almond butter and marmalade, our version of"—the word "version" sounded very British— "peanut butter and jelly." He gave a small laugh.

But Aunt Evie blinked her eyes at him, a way she had of blinking her eyes when she sort of disapproved of something. "Is it on whole wheat bread?" actually making a joke but it went right over the waiter.

"Actually, it is," the waiter said, who smiled again and then got a tiny bit flustered.

Tess jumped in. "We've been to England before," Tess

said brightly, "and we're fine with the grown-up version. Are there petits fours and scones and Devonshire cream?"

"Yes, of course," he said.

"And little egg salad sandwiches?" she asked.

Aunt Evie said, "Lovely."

"And I'll even eat cucumber with butter," said Max. "I'm awfully hungry from the park!"

"Grown up it is. We also have a selection of éclairs and chocolates."

"Really?" said Max. "That's very exciting, isn't it Tess?"

But Tess wasn't paying any attention to him. She had turned her head and was distracted by the boy at the table behind them. The boy smiled at her which made her feel a little shy, but she smiled back. And then he proceeded to—almost as if he was an artist on view, not quite per-formance art but definitely creative—with a magician's precise sleight of hand, and an interesting architectural eye, he started to pile petits fours onto petits fours, using éclairs as walls, tea biscuits as windows, and tea sand-wiches as tiles for a roof, and constructed a very interesting rendition of a house with a blueberry for a doorknob and a sprinkling of Devonshire cream on the rooftop as if it had just recently snowed. It was quite a remarkable creation. And it seemed to Tess to be a show for her. Tess smiled and quietly laughed and turned away so as not to draw attention to him. She didn't point it out to Aunt Evie or Max. It was kind of like it was their secret, hers and the boy who was sitting at the other table.

"The curried turkey is delicious," said Aunt Evie. "Really, you should both try it."

Tess took a bite just to appease Aunt Evie, quite certain she wasn't going to like it, but she was surprised—it had raisins in it and walnuts and chutney.

Tess turned back for a second to the boy sitting alone at the table. It was almost as if she'd imagined the house which was made of confections and tea sandwiches and had white drizzled snow made out of Devonshire cream. The entire concoction had disappeared and everything was back in its place, the sandwiches laid out on the silver platter and set out on his plate as they had been at first.

The waiter arrived again, causing Tess to turn back to their table, as he wanted to know if everything was to their satisfaction and they didn't want to order anything else.

"No, it's lovely," said Aunt Evie, "absolutely perfect." Tess obediently took a bite of an egg salad sandwich this time and declared it, "Delicious." And Max just nodded as he had a mouth full of éclair.

After the waiter left, Tess couldn't help it, she turned back around to catch a peek at the boy at the other table, who she was starting to think was quite mysterious and funny.

Now, he seemed to be staring at her, except he wasn't really. His eyes were looking in her direction and she was looking at him, but it didn't seem like they were making eye contact. Maybe he was just spaced out. Max got that way sometimes when he was tired. She'd felt that way right after they'd unpacked. She recognized the mood. The silver three-layered tray was still on the table with more sandwiches piled high and petits fours, scones, jam, and cream, in addition to the amazing assortment already laid out on his plate, not constructed just laid out for eating. But he really didn't seem to have eaten any of them. Not a bite. *Maybe he was waiting for his parents. That must be it. He was waiting for his parents and he'd been taught to be polite. There was something so strange about the way he stared.*

"Do you see that boy, Max?" Tess asked, staring in the boy's direction.

"It's not nice to stare, Tess," said Aunt Evie.

"I know, Aunt Evie. I'm sorry."

"What boy?" said Max.

"That boy sitting over there." Tess nodded her head back in the direction without looking, as Aunt Evie had admonished her for staring.

"What boy?" said Max again.

"That one," said Tess and turned around to look at him, but there wasn't anyone there.

No one, at all. Just a white tablecloth and four settings, as if no one had been there at all.

The waiter was hovering again, wanting to know if they needed more hot water for their tea. *The waiters were very attentive at the hotel. Maybe they'd cleared the table in a snap. Maybe.*

Tess turned back to look at the table again where the boy had been. Spotless, not even a hint of a chocolate or a tea stain. *Perhaps they'd changed the tablecloth in an instant, too.*

"No, thank you," said Aunt Evie to the waiter who was standing at attention. "Everything was perfect. Tess?"

"Absolutely perfect," said Tess without missing a beat.

The waiter started to clear their plates. Tess heard something rustling behind her.

She turned and saw at the now empty table something that seemed to be tapping at the long white tablecloth which practically touched the ground. Tapping might not have been the right word. Tess was sure she saw something darting around under the tablecloth. And then a paw appeared for a moment and disappeared. And then a baby calico cat appeared. It had stripes of orange even down its tail. It was playing with something intently, batting something back and forth, as if it was playing a game.

Tess nodded to Max who was paying enough attention to her, now, to look back at the table. Max smiled.

It was definitely a kitten. It was having an excellent time pushing whatever it was on the ground and jumping a bit to catch up, as the object rolled every time the cat tapped it with its paw.

The cat was definitely visible in the dining room, now, if anyone did look down. And Tess was afraid that in London, cats might not be supposed to be in a dining room, not a public one anyway, and was going to get into trouble any minute—especially if that overly attentive waiter looked down when he came back to clear their tea cups.

Tess reached down to try to pick the kitten up—and the cat thought that was a game, too, and batted the round object directly to Tess. It hit the side of Tess's foot and rolled to a stop. The baby cat ducked back under the tablecloth leaving what looked like a marble on the floor next to Tess's foot.

Tess leaned down and picked it up. She held it up to the light. It was clear glass and had a red swirl in it, along with a tiny patch of black mixed into the swirl.

Tess held the marble up to the light, in order to see it better, and the spiral inside started to spin, as if Tess was spinning the marble, except she wasn't. It was just the inside of it that was twirling, all by itself, strangely, almost the way a screw spins, so the spinning is almost on a diagonal the faster it goes. And it was starting to spin really fast.

She was probably imagining it. She was tired and, she reasoned, her eyes were probably tired, too. No wonder the marble looked like it was spinning—or rather the inside of the marble looked like it was spinning. Tess set the marble down on the tablecloth and it stopped spinning immediately as if it hadn't been doing anything, at all.

Aunt Evie picked it up and examined it. "It's very old," she said and then she laughed. "Hmm," after examining it longer, "it's a cat's eye marble and it was being played with by a cat."

But Tess didn't laugh. She was very relieved the marble wasn't spinning when Aunt Evie picked it up . . .

"It looks as if it's blown glass," Aunt Evie said. "Hand-made. I wonder how old it is." Aunt Evie set the marble back down on the tablecloth and it sat there very still, clear and still.

Tess wondered if the marble belonged to the boy she'd seen sitting at the table. And she couldn't help it, she also wondered if the marble could do anything else besides spin. . . .

"I see you met Ginger," a voice behind them said.

Tess looked up and saw the waiter. "Our hotel cat. She's usually in the library. Shh," said the waiter, "she's not really supposed to be in here. We found her when she was a tiny kitten, tucked away in a laundry basket with no other kittens or cats around. Fed her myself from a bottle at first," he said very proudly. "She's only twelve weeks old and she is a little bit mischievous." He said this word as if it had four syllables in it: mis-chi-ev-ous.

He leaned down gently, deftly put his hand under the tablecloth, and with true skill and confidence, came out with the young kitten resting on his palm. He barely hid the kitten under the lapel of his vest, one leg sticking out and a bit of a whisker and an ear. "Shh," he said again. "I'll be right back," he said to Tess and Max and Aunt Evie. And then speaking to Ginger he said, "It's off to the library with you. And if you're good," he whispered to the cat but loud enough so Tess and Max could hear him, "and you promise not to tell, I'll bring you a bit of chicken and a bowl of Devonshire cream later."

He stood listening. "What? No, of course not," the waiter said, "not curried. Just plain chicken for you. There. Now, say goodbye."

And the waiter scurried off leaving Tess to wonder if he really thought he was having a conversation with the cat or was just doing that for show. Tess and Max couldn't help it. They both started laughing.

Tess looked at the cat's eye marble sitting on the table. It wasn't spinning, now, and she didn't know whether it had been her or the marble, but she was certain it required further examination or at least should be given an opportunity to be reunited with its owner, if she ever did see the boy again. She sort of hoped she might. She very quietly reached her hand out, folded it quickly around the cat's eye marble and deposited it safely in the right front pocket of her jeans.

hiding away

Evie had wanted both Tess and Max to come down to
the restaurant for a proper dinner, but Tess begged off,
saying she was tired, worried she might be getting a cold.
Max had dutifully chimed in, "I'll meet you Aunt Evie.
I've been looking forward to Shepherd's Pie for weeks."
Shepherd's Pie was a particular English dish, a pie filled
with ground meat layered on the bottom with mashed
potatoes and sometimes peas. It was very comforting.

Max was still hungry, even after the enormous amounts of tea sandwiches, scones, and petits fours he'd consumed at tea. And, he didn't want Aunt Evie to eat alone. Their mother said part of Evie's problem was that Aunt Evie spent so much time alone that she was getting good at it, and their mom didn't think that was necessarily a good thing.

Tess liked being alone sometimes. She called it "collecting her thoughts." It was one of the things she didn't like that much about boarding school—that there was *always* somebody around. She'd been known to take walks up the mountain, even if it was cold and snowy, for just this reason. She was happy to be alone in the hotel suite for an hour or so. Someone had built a fire for them in the living room and it was extra cozy even in the bedroom. She took a bath, put her pajamas on, and her slippers. And then she reached for her jeans which she'd thrown over the back of the armchair. She wanted to take a look at the marble that she'd found. She held it in her hand and studied it. It wasn't doing anything, at all. Not at the moment, anyway. It just looked like an old-fashioned marble possibly made out of hand-blown glass with a red circular pattern inside. It was pretty.

She turned the switch for the overhead chandelier so that she would have more light. It, too, was an elaborate thing, with glass prisms hanging from it and an intricate array of light bulbs in the shape of candles, shedding a soft glow. She set the marble down on the coffee table directly underneath the light fixture.

It didn't take more than a moment for the marble to start to act almost like a prism, reflecting (or was it emitting?) straight orange lines, at different angles, but on the same plane, radiating out 180 degrees in the shape of a fan. *Was that what a vector was?*

She couldn't remember. She wished that Max was there to see it. But he'd been so strange (a bit cranky, really, unpredictable) since they'd been in London, who knows what he would say. He might just say she was imagining things.

She wasn't imagining the reflection it cast on the ceiling, the pattern of symmetrical lines. It made her breathless somehow, a little scared honestly. She flipped the switch off for the chandelier and oddly, the marble seemed to hold onto the reflections for a moment, as if it had a power of its own, and then fade, barely lit by the faint glow from the burning light from logs in the fireplace, and then seemingly be at rest again.

Tess tentatively picked the marble up, frightened it might be hot or emit a spark itself. It was a little warm, but she reasoned the fire was lit, and it felt glass-like, just like a marble should. She hid it in the top drawer of the dresser in the bedroom, behind the socks, underneath the box of Swiss chocolates in the shape of dancing bears she'd bought for her Aunt Evie as a stocking present. It seemed a safe place to put the marble—hidden away, partly so that she wouldn't lose it and also, to tell the truth, it kind of made her nervous to keep it out. *What if it spun so fast it hypnotized her or made Max dizzy or moved objects around the room? What if the symmetrical lines were a pathway to . . . she didn't want to think about that, the possibility that it could lead her somewhere else.* Tess had had an experience like this in England before. She knew she was getting ahead of herself here, but putting it in the sock drawer seemed somewhat like a safety measure. She knew she didn't want to throw it away. That didn't even occur to her.

She wondered what Max would say if she asked about the spinning thing the marble had done earlier. He would probably say she imagined it or that it was some kind of gravitational pull or something, and that someone in the room had something it was attracted to—that made sense. Tess made a *Note to self: ask Max if that was a logical theory?*

She crawled into bed and fell asleep without even turning the bedside light out.

Tess woke up at 2 a.m. to find Max lying in the bed next to her on top of the covers, his feet up by her head, his head down at her feet. He hadn't turned the light off either. He had his pajamas on, too. He did that sometimes, lay down at night to talk to her, when he was feeling a little anxious. But obviously he'd fallen asleep, too. Tess switched the light off. And quietly squeezed his big toe which he didn't seem to notice. Tess turned over and went back to sleep. They hadn't said anything to each other but they both wished their parents' plane hadn't been delayed. And also hoped that when their parents did arrive, they'd be holding hands or something.

max confesses

It was quite late when Tess woke up. The clock said 'ten.'
She was alone in the bedroom. She tiptoed into the living
room and Max must have woken up and moved in the
middle of the night. He was asleep on the cot, face-down,
under the covers, with just his forehead touching the pillow.
Tess always admired the way Max could sleep. His head
hit the pillow and boom, fast asleep. Although she had to
admit that she'd done the same thing last night, as well.

There was an envelope that had been pushed under the door. It was on hotel stationery. Tess opened it.

Dear Tess and Max,

I've gone out $shopping$. I've made arrangements for you to sign your name for breakfast in the dining room. Don't start with dessert, please, although the chocolate croissants are lovely. There are games in the library and a game room in the basement! And I've enclosed some pounds for you to use if you would rather wander up the street. But don't go more than a block or two. I'll be back soon and we'll go for an adventure. The address of the hotel is on the back of this envelope if you wander too far and need a taxi to get home.

Merry Merry Merry
Aunt Evie

Aunt Evie had carefully copied the address of the hotel on the back of the envelope by hand underneath the imprinted part that said **Sanborn House**.

"Where do you think she's gone?" asked Max.

"Taking 'Merry Merry Merry' as a clue," said Tess,

"I suspect holiday shopping. You know what Aunt Evie's like."

"She'll take any occasion to shop?!" said Max which came out slightly meaner than he'd meant it, but still.

"Well, no, she told me she wants all of us to have something to unwrap on Christmas morning. I wouldn't be surprised if she came back with a tree to decorate, too."

"Hmm," said Max, who frankly thought he was too old to be decorating trees.

Tess added, almost psychically, "I hope I never feel I'm too old to decorate a tree."

Max gave her a dirty look. He really hated when she did that. "I really hate it when you do that," said Max, unable to stop himself for calling her on it.

"Do what?" said Tess innocently.

"You know," said Max. But then he didn't say anything more because he really didn't want to have a fight.

By the time they were dressed and seated in the dining room, they'd missed breakfast. "Perfect," said Max, who was definitely heading for a bad mood or what their mom would call a bout of crankiness. But Tess asked the waiter if they could have grilled cheese sandwiches and a side of jam, which she thought was sort of clever, and when the waiter agreed that sort of cheered Max up. He also ordered an espresso. Tess was surprised. She'd never seen Max have coffee before. But she realized she didn't quite know what he did in his dorm. The Montreux Academy dorms were not coed and hers was a half a hill away. "A quarter of a mile, to be exact," Max had informed her when they'd first arrived at school in September. "Our dorms are a quarter of a mile away from each other," he told her. "I looked it up on Google Maps."

After a few bites of grilled cheese (which was delicious with a dollop of strawberry jam spread lightly on top) and which they both ate quite daintily, using a knife and a fork, because, after all, they were in London, Max said sheepishly, "I saw him, too."

"What?" said Tess.

"The boy in the tearoom yesterday. I saw him when we first walked in."

"But—" Tess started to say but Max interrupted her.

"But when I looked back, he was gone and it was so strange. . . . Don't be mad. I saw the—the shape in the garden, too. I can't explain it," he said. He'd put his knife and fork down now. "Please forgive me. I was just hoping that maybe we could have a normal vacation. You know. Where nothing really peculiar happened."

Tess was really trying hard not to get mad. Deep

breath. Actually, she was feeling so many things, she didn't know how to compute them. *Max had seen it, too? Seen everything. Well, had he seen everything?*

"And the marble," Tess asked.

Max nodded. "And the marble. Yes. I saw it spinning. All by itself. Just the inside though."

"Well, at least I feel better that I'm not crazy," said Tess. "I'm not sure how I feel about you right now, though."

"I know. I just wanted everything to be normal," said Max.

"But you know strange things happen to us when we go to England," said Tess. "And I don't think it's really my fault."

"I know," said Max. And he had to admit to himself he knew that all too well.

"And do you see anything now?" asked Tess moving her eyes suggestively around the room.

"No," said Max. He was puzzled because he didn't see anything out of the ordinary at the moment.

"Me either," said Tess. "Just checking." And, slightly pleased with herself for pulling a joke on Max, she picked up her grilled cheese sandwich with her hands and took a big bite of it.

Max picked up his grilled cheese sandwich and took

a bite out of it, too. And they couldn't help it, they both started laughing.

But Tess's mind was racing. *Max had seen it, too.*

After a moment, she said, "Did you see him leave?"

Max shook his head.

"Did you see the waiter clean the table? You were staring straight at it."

Max shook his head again.

"Me either," said Tess. And she had no idea what that could mean.

london graffiti & the skatepark

Tess and Max were just about to go out for a walk when they bumped into Aunt Evie getting out of a black cab and also carrying many shopping bags, full to the brim. It was impossible to conceal that they held presents gaily wrapped in festive paper adorned with curled ribbons and glitter and even a candy cane or two on top. She *had* gone holiday shopping. She turned her back on them at once and whispered to the doorman. She gestured to the children—she did still think of Max and Tess as children—as she squeezed a five-pound note into the doorman's hand. "Just ask the bellman to put them in my room, please. They're awfully heavy."

She turned to Tess and Max and said, "And where were the two of you wanting to be going?" sounding a bit English for a second but excited, as if she was, as stated, up for an adventure.

Max had his camera with him. He wanted to take a few pictures for extra school credit in a photography class he was taking. At the moment he was interested in forms and shapes and he thought he might find some interesting sculpture, statues, or elaborate carvings or decorations on the face of a building. He was imagining lions or dinosaurs or birds or a modern architectural sphere in the middle of a square.

"That sounds fun," said Aunt Evie. "Can I tag along?"

"Of course, Aunt Evie," they said, almost in unison, like Tess was just a half a syllable behind Max but they used exactly the same words.

Aunt Evie added, "And also you did bring your skateboard, didn't you Max? I think I may have found a great skatepark we could go to. I know, you probably don't want me watching, but we could go have a look and see if you liked it, and if you did, I'd wander around the neighborhood while you skated."

Max's eyes lit up. He asked Tess to hold his camera for him and he ran back to the room to get his skateboard which he *had* brought with him from Switzerland. When he came back, skateboard under his arm, Tess handed him back his camera and offered to hold his skateboard under her arm so he could snap pictures whenever he wanted.

They only had to walk a block to find an exceptionally beautiful sculpture of a black dragon, ebony colored, but polished so that it almost shone, its wings spread, even though it was standing, its mouth frighteningly ajar. A few blocks later, Tess pointed out two angels to him, elaborately carved, set above the threshold of a private house which Max grudgingly shot, too. Max rounded out his phototaking with a shot of a white wall, the white barely visible, as it was practically covered in graffiti. And then across from it another wall with a different image and landscape.

Some of the graffiti they saw in London was more like street art, real art, rather than spray painted graffiti surreptitiously drawn in the middle of the night the way it was in New York. One of the walls was particularly striking, with a rendition of a snake, hidden, as if by tall grass, and a moonscape above. The opposite wall was filled with children. The images of the children were almost stick figures, but each had its own expression. Max showed the pictures to Aunt Evie and Tess. Aunt Evie squirmed when she saw the snake. "That was a scary wall," she said.

The snake didn't bother Tess particularly. It was the one with the stick figures that struck her to the core, as if it was something she should be frightened of, stick figures with their own expressions. Stick figures that seemed almost to have a personality of their own.

Max thought the pictures were pretty cool and Tess had to admit that was also true.

Aunt Evie stepped out into the street to try to hail a cab.

Tess looked back up at the wall behind her with the child-like stick figures Max had photographed. The sun was out now, and part of the wall was in shadow and part of it was shining brightly.

They quickly bundled into the cab with Aunt Evie who had already told the driver where they were going. It was a longer drive then they expected but they finally arrived at Victoria Skatepark.

Aunt Evie wanted to give them a little time alone. She said she was going to wander down the street, that there was a lovely confectionary store and they knew how much their mother loved candied ginger and also, she'd googled a bookstore. "But," she added, "I won't go far, and you can always call me on the phone," she said, holding up her iPhone with its bright pink case which Evie insisted made it easier to find.

The park also had graffiti art drawn on it, so Max wanted to take a couple more pictures. Tess was still holding his skateboard.

She felt a tap on her shoulder and turned around to see a British boy in shorts, who asked her if she wanted to race him. There was something taunting about the way he asked, almost bullying, and Tess didn't understand why he asked her not Max, aside from the fact that she was holding the skateboard. Maybe it was because he was certain he could beat her. It was almost like a dare.

Tess took a good look at the skatepark. It was concrete and had a deep bowl, like an empty lake bed. There were banks and ledges and sharped raised edges outside the bowl which would be interesting (in the sense of difficult) to navigate. Especially if you'd never skated that park before. It wasn't so much a place for a race as much as it might be for a competition, one that could involve tricks, but maybe he just meant to race her.

Tess was an excellent snowboarder and she could skateboard. She even knew a couple of tricks but she wasn't sure this was a dare she could take. But then the boy's friend came over and said, "Yeah, I figured you wouldn't race him."

And that was all it took. Tess never liked it when people doubted her.

She always wanted to say to them, *Game on!*

Tess studied Max's skateboard. She knew it was a custom job. She'd watched him build part of it. The skateboard itself was covered in stickers and well-used. The wheels were a little small, which Max had insisted made it excellent for park skating, as opposed to larger wheels which are used for sidewalks and city streets. That was about where her knowledge ended. But the wheels were pure pro, so to speak, narrow, made out of white urethane with gold edging, the metal bearings looked as if there were steel, well-oiled, and high-grade, and Max had insisted, "probably the fastest wheels you could have." Yeah, Max had made sure it was a custom job. Tess looked at him for his approval. Max shook his head but then he shrugged, which wasn't a "yes" or a "no."

The two boys had made him a little mad, too. What was the worst thing that could happen? Max didn't want to think about that—the possibility that Tess could get hurt— he figured the worst thing was the boy might beat her. Then Max thought his plan might be to ask for a rematch and beat him himself if he had to, just to keep the score straight. Max was still trying to calibrate his answer.

But Tess beat him to it. She looked at her opponent.

His dark hair cut short, his eyes intently daring her, and she couldn't help it, she answered, "Game on."

Max rolled his eyes. He couldn't believe what Tess had just gotten herself into, and, of course, it was half his fault. He didn't want her to get hurt but he also didn't want her to know that he had any doubts. He raised his pinkie in the air in a show of solidarity. And Tess raised her right hand and gave him an in-air pinkie swear back. And at the same time, gave herself a silent talking to. She knew she had to be brave, secure, and confident in order to win this race or even race it, at all, perfectly balanced, swift, and what her dad would call, "in the moment." No matter what happened, what course the boy took, she would be right there behind him, next to him, and then, she vowed, she would be ahead. *Game on.*

Tess did know a couple of skateboard tricks, not that she wanted to pull them out of her hat. She knew how to kick flip—when you're skating and you flip the board and land on it again—but she wasn't sure she was going to show that. Their dad had said it was always a good idea to let your opponent underestimate you.

She jumped down to the first ledge and then into the bowl itself. She put the skateboard on the ground and put one foot on it and waited for the boy to join her.

She heard the sound of his skateboard hit the ground and without a signal of any kind, he just started racing. *Game on.*

It only took one round before they cleared the bowl, as if they were dancers whose performance was so extraordinary the other dancers stepped off to watch. He was a speed demon, no question about that, with a very distinct style, using his arms as if he was paddling, as if the air could push him along. But Tess kept pace with him. In a burst of speed, he sailed up, as if he was leading the race and jumped and landed and skated up to a ledge and skated back down again and in an amazing feat, landed back in the bowl and continued to race.

She held back and watched him for a minute, unsure of his moves or his pace and then raced up the bowl herself and executed an astonishing leap at the top of the bowl, shooting the board in front of her and landing, then up the step and back down again and couldn't help herself, she executed a spectacular kick flip, aiming the board to land in front of him, performed two cannonball somersaults in the air on the way down, landing perfectly on the board, and racing right beside him in the bowl. *Game on.*

Tess kept pace right along with him, aware that a crowd had gathered and was watching them.

The boy raced fast, gaining lengths in front of her,

and with no warning, shot up the side of the bowl again and landed, board first, and then his feet were planted securely on it on the ground.

Tess was lagging way behind, still racing a half a lap behind in the bowl. And then she felt the wind behind her easing her on, speeding her way. At lightning speed, she began the steep ascent up the bowl and landed perfectly on the ground a step below him. On the ledge above her the boy, a little cocky now, and smiling, flipped his board up to the next ledge. The board sailed forward, and he dropped to one knee, put his hand out to catch himself, and fell forward, flat-out on the ground as the board speeded away without him. Tess resisted the impulse to say: *Game over.*

Max was there to lend a hand to pull him up, which the boy grudgingly took. Tess complimented him on his amazing run. And thanked him for the match and reached her hand out to shake his. That didn't go over too well either. The boy wouldn't take her hand. He wanted a re-match. Tess was almost game, but Max jumped in and apologized and insisted they had to meet their aunt. Max didn't think you should race someone who wouldn't shake your hand when the match was over.

As Tess and Max walked back to the corner, before they

called Aunt Evie, they did something they hadn't done in a while, linked pinkies as they walked, subtly so that nobody would notice, a silent pinkie swear. It wasn't holding hands, but it was a thing they did, a special way they had of telling each other that they had each other's backs.

They didn't have to call Aunt Evie, as they ran right into her on the corner as she was on her way back to them having found a few treasures at the bookstore, an early edition of a Dylan Thomas poetry book which made Aunt Evie very happy, and a bag of candied ginger for their mom.

"How do you feel about Indian food?" she asked Tess and Max. "There's an excellent Indian restaurant just around the corner from the hotel." Tess and Max both liked spicy food. Tess once dared Max to eat an entire hot pepper which he did without even wincing. Although he did ask for a glass of water after he'd finished. There was something exotic and wonderful about Indian food, the different varieties of flavors, spices, even the spinach was delicious, and mango chutney added a sweetness to the heat of whatever spicy dish they might order.

Not meaning to sound British, although he did, Max said, "That would be brilliant, Aunt Evie." And both Tess and Aunt Evie started laughing although neither one of them could explain exactly why.

staying up after dinner

When they got back to the hotel after dinner, Aunt Evie confessed to being absolutely exhausted. Tess and Max weren't tired, at all, so they asked if it would be all right if they spent some time in the library, "Maybe playing cards?" Tess said with an inflection that indicated it was a question.

"I think that would be fine," Aunt Evie said. "You have your key, right?" Aunt Evie asked.

"Check," said Max and pulled it out and showed it to her.

"And you promise you won't stay up too late?"

"Check," said Tess. And Max nodded in agreement.

"I think that would be all right then," Aunt Evie said. "And hopefully—at least both of them sounded hopeful when they called me this afternoon—your parents will arrive before dinner tomorrow. I made a reservation for five in the dining room at the hotel at eight o'clock, very civilized, if you ask me. I know you already promised, but don't stay up too late, please, and don't eat too many chocolates."

"We promise, Aunt Evie," they said in unison and at the time they said it, they absolutely meant it to be true.

games in the library
and an invitation

There were two young men in the library (which also had a fully stocked serve yourself bar in a small room adjacent to it). The two young men were playing backgammon and drinking red wine.

"Is it just free?" asked Max.

Tess threw her hands up indicating she had no idea. "Why?" she asked. "Were you thinking about having a drink?"

"No!" said Max quite emphatically. "But there's a bottle of Coca-Cola on the counter. And there's an ice bucket. There's also ginger ale which I'm sure Mom would rather us drink at night, right?"

"Right," said Tess. "You pour. I'll have one, too."

Tess opened a cabinet under the bookshelf and found two decks of cards and a board game called Parcheesi. There was a chess board set up in the corner, but Max always won. Max admitted it probably wasn't fun for Tess to play chess with him—Tess could never quite work out what might happen three or four moves from now, which is what Max insisted was the key to becoming any good at chess. She saw Max eyeing the chess board. Tess shook her head.

"What about this?" asked Tess holding up the Parcheesi even though she had no idea what the game was or the rules. . . .

"Most of the pieces are missing," a voice behind them said.

They turned around and saw the boy who had been in the dining room having tea alone. The one who had disappeared. Tess looked at Max to see if he saw him, too. Max nodded.

"It's not terribly fun, anyway," the boy said. And then he added, "I'm Colin, by the way."

"Tess," said Tess.

"Max," said Max.

"Nice to make your acquaintance," he said somewhat formally.

"Are you here for Christmas?" asked Tess, not meaning to be forward.

"I guess so," he said shyly. "Actually, I live here all year round." His voice was soft, with what sounded like a proper English accent, and he seemed exceptionally polite. He was taller than she thought he would be, a couple of inches taller than Tess. He had dark eyes, framed with long dark lashes, delicate features, but a strong jaw that somehow denoted a sense of confidence, and almost the smoothest skin that Tess had ever seen. It was flawless, and he was so pale Tess wondered whether he ever went outside. Then she remembered how little sun there was in London, so it made sense he would be pale. He was a little more dressed than they were, wearing a sort of suit jacket again, but this time a gray one, and those same silver cufflinks. He was a bit of a contradiction, shy and forceful at the same time.

"The pieces have been missing on that game forever," he said, "but I have a table hockey game in my room."

Max's eyes lit up. He loved table hockey. Tess wasn't

sure they should accept what seemed to be an invitation from a stranger. On the other hand, he wasn't exactly a stranger. He was only a couple of years older than Tess, she didn't think, and he was living in the hotel that they were staying at which, Tess reasoned, almost made them neighbors.

"Mother," Colin said, "is having a party but honestly I don't think she'd mind."

Tess looked at Max.

"I mean, it's not like we're leaving the building," said Max.

"I guess that's right," said Tess.

"Thanks," Tess said to Colin. "We'd love to."

party on the 8th floor

Come along then," said Colin anxiously and he led them out of the library into the hall, and pushed the button for the elevator.

When the doors opened, there was an elevator man operating the controls. Tess didn't remember that before. *Maybe that was the policy at night. That made sense. Especially since he looked an awful lot like the doorman. People tended to be security conscious these days, particularly at night.*

"Good evening, James," said Colin quite politely. "I've invited Tess and Max up for dessert and a visit."

James seemed to know Colin very well as he didn't ask for the floor number. He just nodded. The elevator went up one more floor than it usually did. The doors opened on the 8th floor. Max noticed, because he always noticed things like this, that the elevator buttons used to only go to 7. Now, they went to 8. Curious. *It must be a private floor. Had they walked into a different elevator than the one they used yesterday to visit Aunt Evie?* Max and Tess's room was on the first floor, so, he reasoned, he didn't have that much experience with the elevator. But Max could swear the one they were in yesterday only had seven floors.

When they reached the 8th floor and the doors opened, it was even more unusual. The doors opened onto a hallway that only had one door. Not like the rest of the hotel, where there were hotel room doors, lots of them. This just had one door. And it didn't even seem to have a lock, as Colin twisted the doorknob and let them right in. Well, actually, they were let in by what looked like a private doorman. He was dressed in an old-fashioned footman's outfit, a red jacket with gold piping and pants that almost seemed to match. But then again, everyone at the party was dressed up, hair curled in tiny locks around women's over-powdered faces; headbands, some with a flower tied on the right-hand side accenting the gaiety; dresses that fringed; sling back heels. Some of the men were wearing black patent leather loafers that Tess thought looked a little like slippers, but were probably comfortable to dance in, along with their somewhat formal suits; coats with tails; hats; an occasional red or black sash tied around a gentleman's waist; and vests underneath their jackets. It looked almost as if it was a costume party. An effect that was amplified by the piano player performing at the black baby grand piano that was so shiny you could almost see your reflection in it. The top was propped up, for maximum sound level.

The piano player himself was wearing a top hat and a white tuxedo, with a red carnation tucked into the top button of his jacket. But when Tess looked at him closely, she realized it was the same man she'd met wearing the bowler hat in the lobby. Although she didn't see any sign of the white terrier Princess around. He was accompanied by a singer, a very beautiful black woman with a slight French accent singing in a deep, sultry voice, songs about love and loss, to the strangely upbeat piano arrangements of what seemed to be twenties dance tunes. There were waiters in white long-sleeved shirts and red bowties and curiously formal black pants.

"Definitely a costume party," Max whispered to Tess, who wasn't sure that was what it was, at all.

Tess looked down at what she was wearing. She was glad she'd decided to dress for dinner out with Aunt Evie. She was wearing a white dress with a little bit of black smocking up at the top, which made it seem fancier than it was, as it was just a cotton dress with slight elaborate stitching at the top, empire, and not too short, just above the knee. It was cold out, so she'd put on white stockings and then because she felt like it, even though it probably wasn't weather appropriate, she put on a pair of black patent leather Mary Janes that looked like some of the dress shoes the gentleman guests were wearing, so she sort of felt as if she fit in.

Tess was glad Max had decided to wear khakis instead of jeans and a pale blue shirt, even though he didn't match anyone at the party. She decided if anyone asked what he was dressed as, she would jump in and say, "Safari." That would be an answer, for sure.

It felt as if it had been so long ago that they'd gone out for Indian food with Aunt Evie, even though it couldn't have been more than an hour ago. There was something about that elevator ride that felt as if time had elongated, stretched and shrunk at the same time. It was just an elevator ride but when the doors opened, it felt like they were in a different time and place, for sure, light years away or another century. She was letting her imagination run away with itself again. *It was just a costume party.*

The apartment was enchanting. French doors edged the living room and opened onto a terrace with a lovely view of rooftops, some of which were still dotted with snow from the day before. There was a formal dining room but tonight it was being used a bit casually, as a buffet was set up. But there was nothing casual about the display. Fancy English food. Roast beef with the bone in on a sideboard and a waiter in a white coat carving it and offering horseradish or mustard sauce. On the table were silver bowls filled with Yorkshire Pudding, creamed spinach, string beans, and boiled potatoes drenched in butter and decorated with parsley. Tess couldn't help but wonder what was for dessert.

"We've eaten thanks," she said to Colin who then led them back to his bedroom which had a sitting room as well as a bedroom, as if it were his own suite, and sure enough there was a hockey table set up in the sitting room.

Tess sat on the couch and watched quietly as Max

and Colin played an incredibly competitive game of table hockey until a strange thing happened. Max whacked the puck back at Colin fast, so that it practically flew, sliding across the table missing all the paddles. But Colin didn't seem to be paying attention, at all. It was as if he was just standing there, possibly not seeing, or not seeing them, or not seeing the round puck sliding toward him at breakneck speed across the table. It was very strange. It seemed to Tess that Colin was almost, well, mesmerized wasn't the right word, but it was as if he was fixed in space for a moment.

Max's cries of "hurrah" as he'd won the game seemed to bring Colin back to earth. Tess wondered what he could have been thinking about so hard, because she assumed *that* was what it was, that Colin had become lost in thought, which is not a good idea in the middle of a competitive sports match especially if you're one of the players.

Colin conceded the game, somewhat elegantly. "Well done!" he said sounding very English. And then asked Tess if she wanted to play her brother. It was as if he'd skipped a beat in time, hadn't been aware of the fact that he'd sort of been frozen for a moment or less elegantly put, spaced out.

Tess shook her head. She didn't think she wanted to take a chance at the hockey table.

"There are lovely desserts, I bet, put out by now," Colin added, which sounded excellent to Max and Tess, especially Tess as she could hear the live music from the living room, laughter, and the tinkling of ice. Tess was always one for dancing, or at least watching it, if dancing itself wasn't on the table.

CHAPTER ELEVEN

Sliding through the party

Tess and Max felt almost invisible as they went slinking through the party. The women, in four-inch heels and antique party dresses, and the men, in formal suits, were all engrossed in conversation or swaying to the music. In the dining room, silver trays were piled high with desserts and displayed on the buffet table.

Max quietly linked his pinkie to Tess, subtly down at their waists. A secret pinkie swear which meant they had each other's backs. Although neither Tess or Max was sure what was making them feel cautious and shy. Certainly, they didn't know anyone besides Colin although Tess had met the man in the bowler hat, who was now wearing a top hat as he played the piano, but it was more than that. . . . They were each feeling that they didn't belong.

Tess wondered if Colin felt that way, too, although she doubted it, as he led them so effortlessly through the crowded party, stopping for a moment to smile at someone and in one case kiss an older woman's hand. There was something so affectionate and respectable about it, Tess wondered if it was his aunt or his mother's best friend or someone royal. That was the theory she liked the most. Everyone was so elegant. It felt to Tess as if, somehow, she and Max had faded and the rest of the party was in bright Kodachrome, an old kind of film that Max had learned about in photography class, where colors were almost brighter as if they'd been enhanced.

The jewelry alone sparkled, particularly the diamond necklace on the neck of the woman who came up to greet them and kiss Colin on the top of his head. Her light brown hair, tousled in pin curls around her face, the shape of which was almost pixieish, except she was classically beautiful, with dark blue eyes and long dark lashes, a perfectly shaped mouth, accented by soft pink lipstick, rouge on her cheeks which were framed by elegant and delicate cheekbones, and a lovely dimple on the right side of her mouth when she smiled, which she did when Colin introduced them to her and explained that she was his mother and her name was Janice Sanborn.

It occurred to Tess that her last name (and presumably Colin's) was the same as the hotel's, **SANBORN HOUSE**, and wondered if that meant they had a connection to the hotel or to the family who owned the hotel. Or they were the family who owned the hotel? *It could explain why they had the entire top floor and a private entrance. That made sense.* Tess was feeling a little bit like Max at the moment—she found it comforting when things were logical.

Colin's mother only stayed with them for a moment, after suggesting they try the trifle which she said was lovely, as the strawberries were fresh, and "Be sure," she added softly, "to add extra whipped cream. I'm so happy," she added, "that Colin has found two friends." And then she bustled off, leaving behind the slightest scent of a light perfume, as she walked back into the living room where the dancing was in full swing.

The trifle was delicious and so were the chocolates

and the butterscotch candy that Colin made Tess try, even though she was quite full. Colin didn't eat anything, at all, saying he'd had dinner earlier in the kitchen.

He led them into the living room, too, where Tess had a lovely view of the dancers, who were wild and skilled and elegant at the same time, effortlessly performing back dips and over the shoulder moves, one young gentleman lifting his partner and practically tossing her over his shoulder and then sliding her back, gracefully onto the ground, which required both to perform their moves in perfect step with one another. There was a little bit of tap dancing here and there. Some of the dancers seemed as if they were trained. It occurred to Tess that maybe everyone in England took dancing lessons when they were a kid.

Colin introduced them to his sister, too, whose name was Elizabeth and who was eight. And, as the music crescendoed at exactly that moment, Colin playfully took Elizabeth's hand and gave her a tiny bit of a dance spin in the room, which despite her age she pulled off rather elegantly. And then laughing, Colin took Tess's hand and gave her a spin, too, which she executed brilliantly. But he was a very good dancer. It only lasted a minute, as the music ended.

On the other side of the dance floor, there was a line of

people waiting to talk to a young woman who was seated behind a table. She, too, had pin curls and she was wearing white satin ballet slippers and a lovely, white satin dress with sleeves that puffed like a princess's. Her eyes were dark and she was sitting in a wing-backed chair in front of a small mahogany side table that had been placed in front of her. On the other side of the table was another chair that was presently occupied by a tall young gentleman, who was holding his right hand out, palm up for the young woman to see.

"That's Adele," said Colin quietly. "She's a 'seer.'" And then he added almost in a whisper, "My mother believes in 'seers' and so do most of her friends."

Tess didn't say anything at first. She wanted to say that she knew someone like that, too, not like his mom, like Adele. But Max gave Tess an intense dirty look as if he was begging her telepathically not to say anything, at all.

But then Tess couldn't help herself entirely. "I want to talk to her," she said excitedly. "Colin do you think your mother would mind if I asked for a reading, too?"

"Not at all," said Colin. "I'm sure she'd approve of it."

Max just rolled his eyes.

reading the cards

Do you want me to tell you something you already know?" Adele asked. Tess was now seated opposite her, the mahogany side table between them.

It was such a strange question. "Why would I want you to tell me something I already know?" asked Tess, confused by Adele already.

Adele laughed. "Sometimes people like reassurance," she answered. "And sometimes I tell people things they already know. It's not me really. I ask the question, or you do, but it's the cards that tell me the answer. I'm not much more than a conduit," she said modestly.

Tess looked at Max for an explanation. "A conduit is something that conveys things," Max explained, understanding what Tess was asking without her even posing the question. "Sort of like a pipe is a conduit for conveying water."

"You did want a reading of the cards, didn't you?" asked Adele.

Tess wasn't sure what she wanted.

She knew she didn't want her palm read—that felt too definitive. She knew she didn't want to throw coins or that other thing that they called runes, bamboo sticks, that their mom's friend Franny liked to throw. That felt like taking too much of a chance.

But suddenly Adele had a deck of cards in her hand. They seemed to appear out of nowhere. The back of the cards had stars and a moon and a planet that looked like Saturn with a ring around it and in the top right, a picture of a profile of a woman who looked a bit like Adele herself. The back of the cards was navy-colored and the stars, moon, and Saturn were painted in white, as was the picture of the face of the lady, which had a circle around it, so that her face was framed like a cameo.

Tess figured if Adele had a deck of cards with her own face painted on them that maybe she was legit, but she wasn't sure she could back up that logic. That could be part of the show, too. She was sure though that it wasn't a coincidence that the face on the cards resembled Adele.

"Cards it is then," said Adele without waiting for an answer and expertly flipped three cards up and placed them next to each other in a straight line.

Adele looked down at the cards and then up at Tess, as if she was examining her. Then Adele's eyes fluttered. When she opened them, she seemed to be not really looking at Tess, even though she was staring straight at her.

Her voice sounded strange as if it was coming from a distant place. It occurred to Tess the whole thing might really be a performance, a very practiced act. Except Tess couldn't quite figure out how Adele was making her voice sound as if it was coming from a hushed megaphone, whispered and amplified at the same time. It was *very* strange.

"You know there's something on the other side of the wall, don't you?" Adele said simply.

Actually, Tess didn't know that, at all, but before Tess could reply, a voice behind them piped in softly, "Oh Adele, are you frightening the children again? I asked you not to do that."

Adele fluttered her eyes, as if she'd been in a trance or something.

"She once told me the strangest thing," said Colin's mother to Tess. "It was as if she was in a trance or something. She said, 'How do rats know when houses are empty?' I had no idea what that meant. Adele, really," said Colin's mother. "I mean it, you're not supposed to frighten the children!"

"I wasn't meaning to Mrs. Sanborn. Not at all," said Adele. "It's the cards that tell me what to say. You know that."

"You do know that, Mother," Colin piped in. "Or at least you believe it. My mother hardly makes a move without consulting Adele," he said to Tess and Max. "Never a big decision without her."

His mother laughed which was sort of refreshing as Tess thought Colin might be making fun of his mother.

"It's true. I don't. Adele is a bit of a wonder. But I do hope she hasn't told you anything too startling." She tousled Colin's head again and practically danced back into the party.

Somehow Tess couldn't shake it. It was a warning. There was no question about that. *You know, don't you? There's something on the other side of the wall.* That's

73

what she'd said, really, wasn't it? That Tess knew there was something on the other side of the wall. Was that what Adele meant when she said she was going to tell Tess something she might already know? *Was that what she was referring to? Or was it something else?*

Colin's mother had interrupted her reading. Tess had tried to hang around by the table, but another woman had already sat down for a reading. And it was one a.m. and Max insisted they had to go back down to their suite.

They thanked Colin and he said he was awfully glad they'd come and he seemed to mean it. It had been sort of fun. Memorable even. Tess's mother said those were the best nights out, the ones that you remember.

Colin politely walked them out to the elevator which arrived this time without an elevator operator.

Max did not point out to Tess that there *were* only 7 numbers on the elevator panel, even though he did note it himself. Tess was weirded out enough already. Tess didn't usually get unsettled by anything. Max was also tired. He hoped Aunt Evie hadn't "checked" on them. It was late, and he was certain she would be nervous if she hadn't been able to find them. But thankfully everything was copacetic in The Garden Room. "Copacetic" was a funny word their mom used—it meant A-OK. In less than four minutes, both Tess and Max were in their pajamas and in their beds, safely under the covers, sound asleep.

Tess had a dream she was trying to make her way through a maze, high-tech, orange-colored and strangely three-dimensional, straight waves of Day-Glo orange light, precise lines in a hallway that sharply changed direction and elevation in a nanosecond and seemed to have no end. She wasn't certain whether she was supposed to be walking on them, as if they were a pathway, or underneath, ducking endlessly below them, sidestepping them, for fear they were a laser of a sort or a sophisticated security system that might sound an alarm at any moment, as if she wasn't meant to be there, at all.

She was startled awake by the dream. Her heart was pounding. The dream ended—well, it hadn't really ended. She'd woken up in the middle—without her knowing whether she'd found her way out or not. And the three-dimensional orange lines reminded her of the strange vectors of light she'd seen that afternoon that had flashed out from the cat's eye marble. It took her a little while to calm down before she went back to sleep.

in which tess hopes that everything is normal

Oatmeal, please," said Tess. There was something comforting about oatmeal. Comforting and normal. "No, no almond milk. Whole milk, please," she said to the waiter who was hovering over her as he always did. He pulled her napkin out from around her silverware and with a flourish settled the napkin on her lap. Tess managed a smile, but she wasn't in the mood to be special or to be treated as if she was special.

She realized she was starting to feel a little like Max had, wishing they could have a normal vacation. She was still a bit shook up from the dream she'd had the night before. And the strange thing Adele had said to her that she didn't want to think about.

She was also puzzled by their new friend Colin, the costume party, and his mother's apartment on the 8th floor.

Aunt Evie had said it was a fancy hotel even though it didn't look that way. The sofas in the library were well worn, as were the carpets in the dining room, the drapes in their suite were red velvet, elegant but also ancient. But the party at Colin's mother's apartment had convinced Tess that it was in fact an upscale hotel. 5 Star for sure. Maybe 4.

When they woke up the next day, it was pouring, and the rain showed no signs of letting up. Aunt Evie had looked it up on her iPhone and the weather channel said it was also raining buckets again in Berlin. Actually, it didn't say "buckets." Aunt Evie had added that part for effect when she told Tess and Max. She wasn't sure if their parents *were* going to make it today. Not even because of the weather in Berlin—but London was so windy and wet, there was talk that Heathrow might be shut down for the night if the storm kept up. As if in punctuation, there was a hint of lightning flashing out the window of the dining room, lighting up the dark gray sky. Max counted one . . . two . . . and didn't make it to three before thunder seemed to almost rattle the building.

"Oh, my," said Aunt Evie. "I'm glad we all decided to sleep in."

Aunt Evie wanted to know what they'd done last night after she'd gone to bed.

Max looked at Tess who was excellent at telling stories and leaving out parts that might make people nervous but leaving in parts that were true.

"Max made a friend," said Tess.

If you'd asked Max, he would have said that Tess had made a friend. But he let her continue.

But she corrected herself. "Max and I made a friend," she said. "Colin. Colin Sanborn," said Tess, as she knew Aunt Evie liked them to know a person's first and last name. "Strange. It's the same name as the hotel," Tess said to Aunt Evie. "In fact, he lives in the hotel," Tess added. "All year-round."

"I've always thought it would be lovely to live in a hotel," said Aunt Evie dreamily. "Your bed would be made every morning. Leave your dry cleaning outside the door and magically it would come back to you the next day. If you went out, a hotel operator would take a message for you. You'd have a little box behind the reception desk with your messages in it and any hand delivered packages. You could pick up the phone," Aunt Evie went on, "and order room service, assuming, of course, the hotel you stayed in had room service. . . ." This last was said with a bit of an edge.

That was one of the peculiarities of THE SANBORN HOUSE. It didn't have room service. But Aunt Evie said they got a good deal on the rooms and she didn't mind that much, on this vacation. It was a real holiday and she thought they'd want to all have their meals together. Especially when their parents arrived. *If they ever did arrive.*

"With his parents?" asked Aunt Evie.

"Whose parents?" said Max who had sort of lost the train of thought.

"The boy you made friends with who lives in the hotel."

"Oh," said Tess, jumping in. "We only met his mother. We met his sister, too. She was eight and very adorable. His mother was very elegant, and she was having a costume party."

"Really?" said Evie. "Were people wearing masks?"

"No," said Tess. "But there was a piano player and a singer, and dancing, and everyone was wearing clothes that looked like they might have been from the twenties. And the kid had a table hockey game and Max played table hockey with him and Max won."

"Do you think I really won, Tess?" asked Max. "It seemed like he just stopped paying attention."

"I think he was just—" she hesitated, "—tired," said Tess although she wasn't sure that was true. It had been very strange.

"Is their suite nice?" asked Aunt Evie.

"Oh, no," said Max. "They live on a whole floor."

"Oh," said Aunt Evie. "That does sound lovely. I'm glad you had a nice time."

Tess sincerely hoped that would continue to be the case.

As if in further punctuation, there was another bolt of lightning outside illuminating both the sky and the dining room.

Max counted again. One . . . two . . . and again, he didn't make it to three before the bolt of thunder hit, loud and rolling, and the walls of THE SANBORN HOUSE seemed to shake.

an incident in the garden room

Max was carrying four books. An amazing copy of a book he'd never known existed, *The Lost World* with beautiful illustrations and a plot description that seemed like it might really be the basis for the crazy dinosaur movie he liked so much. It was written by Sir Arthur Conan Doyle who'd written the Sherlock Holmes books. Max thought it was a pretty cool discovery and might be a lovely book to get lost in. He was also carrying a big encyclopedia Tess had found (and borrowed) called *The Encyclopedia of Birds in England* which she thought Aunt Evie might like, and another book Tess had asked him to take down from the shelf, which really didn't make any sense to Max. It was called *Beginning Physics*. Max figured it had been left behind by a hotel guest who was a student, although why Tess was suddenly interested in physics did baffle him and made him a bit nervous. Tess insisted they borrow a dictionary, too. The books were heavy and unwieldy, so when they got to the room, Max handed Tess the key so that she could open the door for them.

Tess felt a spark the moment the key touched her hand. She looked to see if it was sparkling. It wasn't exactly sparkling. Well, maybe she saw a couple of sparks. And a couple of lines, like sparks, orange-colored lines emitting from the crystal handle that looked like the marble she had found. She hoped Max hadn't noticed the sparks.

And then, as if the key had a mind of its own, it magically (or magnetically) seemed to be drawn to the lock. There was a distinct click as it locked in perfectly without Tess even aiming for the keyhole. Then odder still, the key seemed to turn all by itself. Tess was still holding on to it. So, she reasoned, Max wouldn't necessarily know that it turned by itself. But when Tess looked back at him, she knew immediately from the look on Max's face that he had seen it, too.

The door to The Garden Room flew open.

The room looked different, lighter, as if it had been remodeled. Maybe the sun was just out for a change and they'd pulled the curtains back. The sun *was* out and the housekeeper seemed to have opened all the curtains and tied them with sashes. Funny, Tess hadn't noticed that there were sashes before. And, truly, a moment earlier, it had been storming out. Absolutely pouring rain. She didn't think winter storms were like that.

The room looked fancier, somehow. Maybe she'd never seen it in bright daylight. Well, maybe it had changed a bit. Or it hadn't. There was definitely more lace on the pillows on Max's rollaway in the living room. Maybe housekeeping *had* been in while they were at breakfast and changed the sheets. The rug looked newer. That was probably the effect of the light, too. It was the same rug, but it looked newer. And the coffee table was very polished, almost as if you could see your reflection in it.

She was quite startled when a boy's voice said, "Hello."

Colin was sitting on the living room couch as if he belonged there and didn't realize he was intruding and that nobody had asked him in. Although he guessed it from the look on Tess's face.

"I'm so sorry," he said. "Mother says I shouldn't drop in on friends just because they're staying with us. That I'm not supposed to go into their rooms unless I'm asked. It's so peculiar though to have people staying with you, that I always forget. And I wanted to see you both."

"Really?" said Tess, attitude in full force. "And how *did* you get in?"

Tess didn't think people were supposed to walk into your hotel room uninvited even if, as he seemed to indicate, they owned the hotel. Especially if you aren't even there when they drop in.

"How did you get in?" she asked again accusingly.

"You left the garden door unlocked," said Colin, quietly and sheepishly. "I was playing there. And—and I wanted to see you both. And I touched the handle and it opened. And . . . I'm so sorry. I was just about to leave you a note."

There was a piece of hotel stationery on the table in front of him. And a fancy fountain pen. The stationery was embossed and it said **SANBORN HOUSE** at the top. Just that, no address, no phone number, no email. Tess had noticed this before and thought it was sort of cool, like a printed note card. The stationery was very white, almost like parchment paper. And Tess had seen the envelopes for it, just the right size, in the desk drawer. On the back of the envelope was the same embossed name **SANBORN HOUSE**, also with no address below it. Fancy.

But Tess wasn't sure how she felt about Colin yet. He was sweet, interesting, polite, intriguing, for sure, but there was something sad about him that she couldn't quite put her finger on, fragile somehow. She also thought it was very cheeky of Colin, rude in fact, and inappropriate to have let himself into their room.

And, she had to admit, it had sort of been her own fault. Tess had left the garden door unlocked that morning, when she'd poked her nose out to see how cold it was and discovered it was pouring buckets. *Note to self: always lock the garden door. Even in the day-time.*

But then Colin seemed so sad. "I've offended you," he said. "I didn't mean to," he added. "Mother thought we could take the carriage out and I could show you around. If your aunt approved that is."

Max's eyes lit up. Maybe he was going to see the Changing of the Guard, after all. And it did look as though the sun was shining. Max set all the books down on the floor by the desk. "I'd like that, Tess," he said and sat down next to Colin.

There was something strange about the way Max and Colin looked when Tess saw them sitting on the couch, right next to each other. It was as if they were in a different dimension from each other. Not exactly. They were sitting right next to each other, but it didn't seem as though their arms were touching, even though they were so close to each other and Max had a habit of using hand gestures. It was weird. As Tess looked at them, from her vantage point, it seemed as if they'd both been in the same picture, in a magazine or something, or a photograph, but someone had ripped it and when they'd put it back together it didn't look as if they (or the couch) were quite in sync or at the right angle. As if there was a distortion or a distance between them that couldn't be bridged. Even though it looked as if they were sitting right next to each other. It was odd.

Tess shut her eyes for a moment because she knew she was imagining things. She remembered she'd had a headache that morning when she woke up so maybe her eyes were just tired. She hadn't had a lot of sleep the night before.

But then she looked over at them and it got even stranger still. Colin was very pale. Almost paler by the moment. "Are you all right?" asked Tess.

The boy didn't answer. He just got paler still. "Are you all right, Colin?"

Max reached out to touch him, but it was as if his hand seemed to go right through Colin's arm. As if he had become transparent or he wasn't really there, as if . . .

Max jumped up from the couch, scared, as if it was something he could catch. Frightened, as he felt a cold shiver of fear running up his spine.

Colin got paler still. More transparent, as if he was almost fading from view.

Max stepped back even further, as if he was trying to get away.

Colin stood up from the couch, so pale. Translucent, almost as if he was in a trance, smiling so strangely. He started to walk towards Max, purposefully, step by step, directly to him, almost as if Colin was playing chicken or else he wanted to whisper something to Max. That was the only thing Tess could figure out anyway, at first.

But then there was the most startled look on Max's face . . . as Colin walked directly into him and simply disappeared.

Max felt really strange for a moment, as if he had a wrench in his stomach, as if he'd swallowed cold ice. He almost doubled over. Tess ran to his side.

There was no sign of Colin anywhere.

in which max has no idea what's happened to him

Tess seemed to be yelling at him, "Max, Max! Are you okay?!" But he had absolutely no idea why she'd be yelling.

"Of course, I am, Tess," he said. "Why would you think I wasn't?"

Tess didn't know how to explain this next part.

He was standing upright now, as if nothing whatsoever had happened to him.

Tess was frightened. She felt a tear run down her cheek.

"Oh, Tess. Don't get upset. You know I can't bear it when you're upset. And we're on vacation." He smiled. His face looked softer somehow. As if he'd lost that growl he'd been wearing for the last few days, as if his crankiness had worn off.

Not outside though. It was suddenly gray again, amped up by a huge crack of lightning that lit up the sky, like a jagged streak, above the garden trees. She waited for Max to count which he didn't. So Tess did, picking it up at two . . . three . . . four . . . five . . . And then finally the sound of thunder although it seemed to be faraway. The rain wasn't. It was suddenly pouring again, like it had been in the morning.

"Colin," said Tess. "Are you hiding?" She realized he really had disappeared.

"No," said Max, "didn't you hear him? He said he was going to ask his mother if we could take the carriage out which might be lovely, even if it is raining. We could put on galoshes and raincoats."

Tess started laughing. Max looked at her puzzled. She'd never heard him use the word "galoshes" before. But Max clearly didn't get the joke.

"I didn't hear him say he was leaving to go and ask his mother," said Tess.

"I did. Most definitely," said Max sounding slightly British when he said it. Tess wondered if he was playing with her. Putting on a British accent.

But in her mind, all she could think was that she hadn't seen Colin leave. All she'd witnessed was Colin get unbelievably pale, almost translucently pale. She'd seen Max get up from the couch and move away, as if he was oddly frightened and needed to get away. She'd watched as Colin got up and walked towards Max and . . . She had to be imagining things.

"I didn't get a lot of sleep last night," Tess said out loud. "My head hurts. I had a strange dream last night."

"I hate strange dreams," said Max. "I wish they were something you could wish away. Or rather, wish not to have." This last sentence was said with a lot of enunciation between the words, spaces between the last four: wish not to have.

Tess looked at him strangely. Max didn't usually say "Or rather." That wasn't one of his expressions. It was that weird British tone again. She'd also never heard Max say he believed if you wished not to have something, it might have an effect. Max believed in more logical things. Tess looked curiously at Max.

"Are you feeling all right?" asked Tess.

"Yes, quite," he said, sounding even more British when he said this. And Tess couldn't help it, partly out of stress, she started laughing.

Max laughed, too, although he wasn't at all sure why they were laughing.

max

Tess shut her eyes and saw spots, bright colored spots, pink, yellow, blue, almost like bubbles.

Is that what a migraine was? Their mom's best friend Franny got migraines and had to lie down in the dark because she said she saw spots in front of her eyes.

Tess wasn't certain that was what it was, as Franny said she saw them when her eyes were open.

When she opened her eyes, Max was sitting on the

floor, his legs crossed in an almost yoga-like position. Max didn't usually sit on the floor, not unless they were playing a board game or something. Tess had never seen him sit cross-legged. It, too, was like something Franny would do, and she would probably have a name for it, like the lotus position. That was what it was. But Max didn't do that. Max sat in chairs or stood up, or if he was on the floor, he would be sprawled out, at least one leg behind the other and one elbow down, never cross-legged.

Tess shut her eyes again. The spots were still there, pink, blue, orange, almost like confetti, except confetti dropped like waterfalls and these were stationary, as if they were floating in the air, fixed in the black three-dimensional space that presented itself when her eyes were closed, wherever that was . . .

Tess quickly opened her eyes again.

Max was still sitting on the floor cross-legged. Really cross-legged like his right leg was resting on his left thigh and vice versa, like a full-out yoga position. Lotus, for sure.

"I've never seen you sit like that," said Tess.

"You haven't?" said Max as if he was surprised by the question. "I sit this way sometimes. I think it's very—" he hesitated, looking for the right word, "—relaxing."

Tess wondered if Max had taken up meditation, too.

Their dad sometimes meditated. Tess understood that. Their dad's job could be difficult. He had to maintain an aura of calm during his research and on camera. Tess imagined it could be very stressful to be imbedded with the troops in foreign countries and that he had to appear externally at ease and ready to act at any moment. She realized "act" had two meanings: "to act" as in to do something, and "to act" as in to play a part.

And it occurred to Tess, although she couldn't exactly explain why, that Max might actually be acting.

There was a knock on the door.

Before Tess could start to walk over to answer it, Max said, in a very British accent, softly and matter-of-factly, "No one will ever believe you, you know. If I were you, I wouldn't say anything, at all."

CHAPTER SEVENTEEN

an inside-out afternoon

As Tess neared the door, she turned back to glance at Max who was now standing up and looking as normal as could be. She hesitated at the door, unsure of who might be on the other side. But then she heard Aunt Evie call, "Yoo hoo!"

Tess tentatively opened the door.

Tess wasn't entirely sure what she was afraid of but Max or "the person who used to be Max" which is what she was going to call him from now on or at least until she could figure out how to undo this . . . (whatever this was) was absolutely right. There was no way she could tell anyone what she thought had happened because nobody would believe her. At least not anybody she could think of at the moment, who was anywhere around. . . . Except Colin who at this moment in time, she decided she didn't like very much. *Why would Colin want to betray her that way? Why would he have wanted . . .* She couldn't even think about what she thought had happened. All she wanted to do was scream out, "Max!!" and hope that somebody answered her.

"Yoo hoo, yourself," said Tess to Aunt Evie, trying to sound cheery. Evie was wearing her boots and coat.

"You won't believe it," Aunt Evie announced, "the hotel just called. They didn't want us sitting around all day, so they've given us the house car and we can go anywhere we want."

"The carriage?" asked Tess.

"No, not the carriage. An actual car and driver. The concierge said he hoped we had an excellent adventure."

Tess hoped so, too, as she realized, that even though Aunt Evie didn't know this, that the adventure had already started.

Almost in a nanosecond, Max put on his boots, his ski hat, his down coat, and gloves.

Tess hadn't even made it to the closet yet, let alone her bedroom to the drawer where she usually kept her gloves, except that they weren't where she usually put them.

Max blinked at her as she raced around, actually unable to find her gloves. "I think they're under the sofa," said Max, brightly, as if he was trying to be helpful.

Tess gave him a dirty look. But he was right. They were, in fact, under the sofa. "Thanks," she managed.

"Well, come along then," said Aunt Evie. "If we hurry we can hear Big Ben."

"I'd like that," said Max, "I hear the Gothic architecture is amazing."

"Yes, I'm sure you would," said Tess. "But don't you remember Max, we looked this up on your computer at school, as you were interested in the clock, too? Big Ben's closed for renovation. The building's closed and the bells will be silent until sometime in the 2020's when the renovation is done."

"The person who used to be Max" gave her a surprised look. Tess could play, too. In fact, that's what she thought to herself, *Game on.*

"Of course," he said instantly. "I'd forgotten that."

in which princess pays a visit

Max was being sweet as pie. He was lying on top of the covers on the rollaway bed. He'd even taken his boots off, lying flat on his back with his feet crossed, strangely at rest, and acting extremely un-Max-like. Tess was almost beyond cranky. It had rained the whole time they'd been out in the car. They'd stopped at the big department store Harrods, but it was so crowded with holiday shoppers that it wasn't fun either. Finally, Aunt Evie decided they should all go home and have a nap.

Max turned and gave Tess a sweet, slightly sarcastic smile. She almost wanted to slap him.

It occurred to her that she should go for a walk and calm down. It was still raining. But she'd promised her mom that she and Max wouldn't fight. That didn't necessarily apply to "the person who used to be Max" but she wasn't sure her mom would agree.

Then the idea that *she* had to leave the room upset her. It was Tess's hotel room, too, and what she referred to as "the person who used to be Max" was lying self-satisfied on the cot, weirdly reading *The Encyclopedia of Birds*, a subject that had never interested Max. His fake smiling at her was making her so irritated that she felt she had to leave her own room.

She was frightened she might snap at him, have an encounter with him, and she didn't know where that could lead. . . . The truth is, she was a little frightened of him. Frightened and confused. And hurt and betrayed.

As if in punctuation, "the person who used to be Max" gave her another sweet, treacly smile, strangely evil, that almost did make her want to slap him. She wondered if that would work. If she slapped him, if Max would come back.

And then, she heard a knock at the door. It was probably Aunt Evie.

As Tess neared the door, she realized it sounded more like a scratching than a knock.

"Who's there?" she called out, but nobody answered. Then the scratching noise shifted into a funny tapping noise outside the door. Tess hesitated.

The tapping kept on. There was definitely someone at the door. . . .

She called out again, "Who's there?" But again, nobody answered.

Tess grabbed the fire poker, just in case . . . Not that she had any idea what she was going to do with it, but she wasn't certain "the person who used to be Max" would come to her aid, if she needed him.

She glanced back at him lying so quietly, almost still, on the cot.

The tapping continued.

Tess looked at the door and shook her head. Everything was so messed up already, at least in her mind. How much *more* trouble could they get into if she opened the door?

In this case, it was sort of a relief, as she didn't see anything at first and then she felt something jostle her feet and she was very happy the funny white terrier Princess had decided to pay a visit.

Tess didn't have to ask her in, as Princess scampered through the doorway and rolled over on the carpet.

Tess laughed and said to Max or to "the person who used to be Max," "It's that sweet terrier I met yesterday."

Was it only yesterday, maybe it was the day before?

Princess still had the pink satin bow tied into a lock of her hair at the top of her head, like a tiny ponytail sticking straight up.

Tess bent down to pet her, but as she did, the terrier Princess disappeared. *Vanished?* That was probably the right word. *Morphed.* It wasn't like there was a "poof" or anything, just gone. And Adele the psychic was standing in front of her.

Ignoring her own rule that it was never a good idea to be rude to a psychic, Tess said, "Is that the custom around here? Really? I do think that people should ask to be invited into a room. I don't even mean that. Doesn't anyone ever call before they stop by?" she added. There was a lot of attitude in Tess's voice.

"I do like to make an entrance," said Adele.

Tess didn't respond to that. She was startled by the way Adele had "appeared" and she realized there was no sign of Princess anywhere in the room . . .

Tess was worried about Max or "the person who

used to be Max." And she didn't know exactly what Adele's purpose or motive might be. She tried to remember her dad's advice. "Keep a calm surface," he'd say, "as if you're relaxed. But always be aware and ready to act at any moment." Tess realized this was one of those moments.

"I'm so happy to see you," Tess said, changing her tone. "You simply startled me. I wasn't expecting to see you again, Adele. It's such a nice surprise. I think the rain has put me out of sorts. I don't have much to offer you," she said. "I have a bag of licorice though. You don't like red?"

"You're quite right," said Adele, ignoring the licorice question. "But I didn't want anyone to see me. You can understand that, can't you?"

Tess nodded.

"And," Adele added, "it was very rude of me to drop in this way. Would you like me to leave?"

"Not really," said Tess. "I'm—I'm glad you stopped by."

It wasn't the first time Tess had seen anybody morph although it hadn't occurred to her that Adele and the terrier Princess were the same being. She wondered what else Adele could do.

Tess looked down to confirm there was no sign of the

little terrier, at all. And oddly, or not so oddly, Adele had a pink satin headband in her hair with a pink bow angled at the side.

"All right, then," said Adele, "I thought you might need some looking after," she said.

Tess had to admit that might be true.

Adele led Tess to the couch and asked Tess to sit down with her.

Tess sat quietly, not saying a word, while Adele took a good long look at "the person who used to be Max."

The boy was standing, very still. He'd put his boots back on. His posture was almost perfect. The look he was giving Adele back was very strange.

The rain had stopped. As if in an instant, the sky had cleared again and there was a view of the moon, almost full, from the top pane of glass in the French doors that led out to the garden and a star shining brightly just above the moon.

Tess wanted to ask Max if the star above the moon was the planet Venus? Max would know the answer to that.

But "the person who used to be Max" announced, as if he was bored with both of them, "I'll be out in the garden." He opened the door and walked out, carefully shutting the door behind him.

Tess didn't tell him to put his coat on. If it was cold, he could figure that out for himself. The rain did seem to have stopped.

The moment the door to the garden shut, Adele said to Tess, "I had a feeling he was going to do this one day."

trying to get to the truth of the matter

I'm not imagining it then, am I?" asked Tess.

"No, my dear," said Adele.

"I would think that he would be afraid of you, though," said Tess, "since you know the truth . . ."

Adele cut in, "Afraid of me? No. Afraid of you, maybe," she added.

"Me?" said Tess as if the idea of that was laughable. I mean, Tess reasoned, she *was* on to him and she was good at playing "the game," as she'd started to call it—catching him on things that were particularly, absolutely, definitively not Max-like. But she also felt she might be playing out of her league. That Colin or "the person who used to be Max" was the one who was actually frightening.

"Yes, afraid of you," said Adele,

"Why?" asked Tess. "Why would he be afraid of me?"

"Because you're the only one who can help him, my dear, and I think he's afraid that you won't."

She looked out the window and saw "the person who used to be Max" swinging on an old-fashioned swing hanging from the white birch tree, framed perfectly in the night light. Tess had never noticed the swing before, but she hadn't spent a lot of time in the garden.

"If he wants me to help him, he's certainly going about it in a strange way," said Tess. And then she asked Adele, "Help him, how?"

Adele hesitated before she answered, "You're the only one who can put him back on solid ground."

"I have no idea how I could help him do that? Can you tell me, at least, how I might do that?" she asked Adele, letting her frustration show for a minute.

But when she looked over at Adele to hear her answer, no one was there. Instead, nuzzling at her feet was the white terrier Princess, the pink satin bow tied into a tuft of hair right above her forehead, like a ponytail, sticking straight up.

Tess resisted the impulse to say something irritable to the white terrier. In truth, she was a little scared of Adele. Especially since she apparently could morph from being a perfectly adorable terrier named Princess to the seer named Adele. Tess did wonder what else she could do. And why she wouldn't help her with Colin.

As Tess watched "the person who used to be Max" swinging on the old-fashioned swing hanging from the birch tree, she could hear him sing a song that sounded old-fashioned, as if it could be accompanied by a chorus, if there were one around, something about "angels dancing in the sky."

It certainly wasn't a song Tess had ever heard before.

Well, at least he was singing about angels. It could be worse, she reasoned. *It could be a lot worse....*

Tess put her hand down and scratched the top of Princess's head.

And there was another knock at the door. Tess answered it, without even thinking. It was the piano player, the gentleman she'd run into in the lobby. He was wearing a topcoat and a hat. "You haven't seen—" but before he could finish Princess ran up to him, waving her tail. "I had a feeling you were going to check on the children.

"Thank you for looking after her, my dear," he said to Tess, echoing the term of endearment that Adele had just used.

"Umm, you're welcome," said Tess who wasn't quite sure *how* she should answer. "Any time." She looked deeply into the terrier's dark almond-colored eyes and Princess stared intensely back at her. It was strange. It was a look of understanding and, Tess didn't want to add, sympathy, more like the way you look at someone when you want to encourage them or believe in them, as if you're proud of them. It reminded her of the way her dad looked at her sometimes.

"You little muffin," he said to Princess and picked the terrier up in his arms. "You know you're not supposed to go running off by yourself." And he walked away leaving Tess to wonder what exactly had just happened.

She locked the door from inside. And before she could even make it to her bedroom to try to decide what dress she should put on (she thought she should dress for dinner since they were eating in the dining room at the hotel and her parents were arriving which in some ways was an extremely comforting thought), there was another knock at the door. But this one was insistent, quite forceful in fact. Three knocks.

Tess walked back to the door and called out, "Who's there?"

"Yoo hoo," was the answer in Aunt Evie's pleasantest voice.

And Tess opened the door again. And Aunt Evie walked into the room.

As she did, "the person who used to be Max" walked in from the garden and said, as if on cue, "Oh, Aunt Evie, is it that late already? Have our parents come? Is it time to dress for dinner? Is it all right if I wear a white button-down shirt with cufflinks?"

Max had never had cufflinks before. At least not any that Tess had ever seen or knew about.

Before Tess could interject, Aunt Evie said, "I'm afraid—" she hesitated as she was upset about this, too. "I have a bit of bad news. So many planes were delayed, that your parents weren't able to get on one today. . . ."

Tess felt another tear drop from her right eye. She wiped it away. She was kind of counting on her mom and dad this time. She wasn't sure she was up to this.

Aunt Evie's voice got softer. "The network got them on a plane tomorrow though. Guaranteed! Your dad wanted to drive. Can you imagine?"

"It's an eleven-hour drive," said Tess. "Max looked it up. Actually, eleven and a half."

"The person who used to be Max" didn't say anything except, "I'll save the cufflinks for tomorrow, then. How do you feel about the blue shirt I have, with the white collar, Tess?"

Tess thought to herself, *What blue shirt with what white collar?* But out loud she said, "That would be lovely." She realized she'd started it this time, with the comment about the length of the drive, but she also realized it might not be the best strategy to play the game right now.

Tess walked into the bedroom, shut the door, took her blue denim dress out of the closet and her black patent leather sandals. She reminded herself to breathe. She couldn't help it: the breath came out sort of as a sigh.

She looked over at the dresser and for reasons that she couldn't explain, went into the dresser drawer and took the cat's eye marble out from behind her socks where she'd hidden it. She set it down on the bedside table, still wrapped in the lace handkerchief. She put on the blue denim dress. And she carefully dropped the cat's eye marble, still wrapped in the lace, into the front right pocket of her dress.

She put her hand on her hip, so that her fingers were over the pocket and she felt a spark, a strange warmth coming, she suspected, from the marble. Somehow, it gave her a feeling of strength, empowerment, although she had no idea what that could mean or how it could be used.

She couldn't help but remember the first thing Adele had told her. *You already know this, but there's something on the other side of the wall.*

Did she? Did she already know it? Taking a page from her dad's handbook, "Take a moment to assess the situation," Tess tried to think of what she really did know.

*in which tess attempts
to assess the situation*

All during dinner, that's what she did.

First, Tess insisted—very politely, of course, saying please, after she saw that the table *was* empty—that the maître d' seat them at the table they'd sat at when she'd first seen the boy sitting alone having tea; the boy who they'd later met in the library; the boy who told them his name was Colin; who invited them up to the 8th floor to his mother's apartment where she was having that amazing party; the boy who. . . . Tess didn't want to finish that sentence.

"We've come to think of it as our family table," Tess told the maître d'.

This wasn't the only reason. She was trying to follow another one of her father's rules. *If you get lost go back to where you started, if you can.* He always added that part, *if you can.* And Tess reasoned that was where it started, when she saw the boy sitting at the table behind her.

Tess noticed that table was empty, too.

"Aunt Evie," she said. "Would you mind if I sat on this side tonight?" Tess wanted a clear view of the table.

The maître d' tried to hide his smile as he pulled the chair out ceremoniously for Aunt Evie to sit down where Tess had directed her.

"We've also become very fond of Fredrik," Tess added. "He's always so nice to us." Fredrik was the hovering waiter, who Tess hadn't liked until he rescued the cat named Ginger and Tess realized the only reason he hovered was because he wanted them to be happy.

"I hereby declare this *your* family table," said the maître d'. "But Sunday is Fredrik's day off. And you will be served tonight by Sonya who I'm quite certain you'll like just as much."

Tess wasn't sure of that. Fredrik was funny, and they'd developed a sort of cozy relationship. And Sonya was a frighteningly fierce-looking woman, tiny, her long dark hair pulled back in a bun, with dark piercing eyes (that weirdly reminded Tess of Adele's).

Sonya had an extremely deep voice. And when she rolled the prime rib over to slice it for them she displayed skills that were magician-worthy. In fact, she put on quite a show with the carving knife, tossing it up in the air and twirling it four times in between each slice, which in itself was terrifying. Tess decided Sonya could probably hit anything if she aimed for it.

Tess resolved to be extra polite to Sonya and to keep her distance, too. But when she asked whether she might have honey with her Yorkshire pudding, Sonya laughed so heartily, and suggested butter as well, that Tess decided maybe she liked Sonya, too.

Tess kept glancing at the table behind Aunt Evie. Nothing. Just a white tablecloth and nobody there.

"The person who used to be Max" ate very little. Tess decided not to assess whether "Max" used more horseradish than usual on his prime rib, except he did. They split a prime rib dinner, as they always had. And split a baked potato. Tess couldn't help but notice that "the person who used to be Max" did not put chives on his baked potato or load it up with sour cream the way Max always had. Aunt Evie noticed it, too, and asked him if he was on a diet. But "Max" answered, "No, just feeling a little woozy, I'm not sure why." *That sounded like Max.*

Tess glanced over at the other table again which was suddenly set for four. *It was so odd.* Tess hadn't seen anyone come to set it. Maybe she'd been paying attention to Sonya's spinning knife show.

There was a lit candelabra in the center of the table, with six elegant candlesticks, ivory-colored, the flames burning faintly, casting an old-fashioned glow. There were two crystal champagne glasses at two of the settings and two matching crystal tumblers, the shape of a glass for water or juice, at the other two. Silver forks, a knife, and a spoon at each place setting.

Inadvertently, Tess put her hand in her pocket and found the glass marble and held on to it. For a moment, Tess was sure she saw four people sitting there, a well-dressed woman who looked a lot like Colin's mother, a well-dressed gentleman who might in fact be his father, a young girl who looked like Elizabeth, Colin's eight-year-old sister, and a boy who definitely looked like Colin, all delicately eating triangles of toast which seemed to be topped by thinly sliced smoked salmon. The woman tousled Colin's head, the way their mom used to sometimes with Max right before she sent him off to school.

Tess heard a piano playing. She turned and saw a black baby grand piano in the corner of the lobby. The top was up, and it was so shiny you could practically see your reflection in it, even from a distance. The melody was catching, almost hip hop but bluesy. The piano player had his bowler hat on and just at his feet underneath the piano was the terrier Princess sitting on a pink satin pillow as if it was her special place. The piano player was accompanied by a young female violinist, whose ability to hit a single note and hold it was almost like a percussion note to the bouncy blues-like song, if a blues-like song can be bouncy. The singer was there, too, and all Tess could catch of the lyrics was something like:

Dancin' into the night now,
Dancing into the night.
I see. I see.
But I'm not sure you want me to tell you what I see . . .

It started out all light and airy, but the last lyric sounded almost like a warning.

Before she could direct Aunt Evie's attention to the lobby, Tess turned back to the table. For a moment, there were only three people there. Colin's mother and what Tess thought was his father and his sister Elizabeth. The boy who might be Colin wasn't at the table any more. And the table was only set for three.

Tess shut her eyes and grabbed the marble tightly as she heard the song lyric repeat again . . .

I see. I see.

But I'm not sure you want me to tell you what I see . . .

She opened her eyes. She realized she was holding the marble really tightly. She let go of the marble and took her hand out of her pocket and as she did the image faded. The table was empty, the candelabra and the four people who had been seated there (or was it three people) were nowhere in sight. The table looked as if no one had been there yet, at all.

Tess turned to the lobby and the grand piano was gone, as well, and so were the piano player, the singer, and the lovely young woman playing high notes on the violin. The terrier Princess was nowhere to be seen.

Tess wondered if she had been imagining it. . . .

"Are you feeling all right, Tess?" asked "the person who used to be Max."

"Yes," said Tess instantly, almost snapping back at him. "Are you? You have been acting a little strangely, frankly. I've never seen you eat a baked potato without chives."

The boy smiled. "I guess I was just in a spirit of invention," he answered.

Tess didn't remark on the use of the word "spirit" although she noticed it. *Was that what it was? The whole phrase was troublesome. A spirit of invention.* Or was she just imagining things?

Sonya brought them dessert. On the house. She said the maître d' had insisted. An elegant bowl of berries for Aunt Evie and two ice cream sundaes for them, two scoops of vanilla ice cream, lightly sprinkled with toasted almonds, and abundantly drizzled with hot Nutella sauce.

Tess watched as "Max" ignored the almonds and the scoops of ice cream and went about carefully scraping all the Nutella sauce, bit by bit, off the ice cream as if it was award winning chocolate fudge sauce and ate it very, very slowly, licking the spoon.

"This is really delicious," said "the person who used to be Max."

Max hated Nutella, or at least he used to . . .

Aunt Evie noticed it, too.

Aunt Evie wondered if Tess knew that while she was

changing into her denim dress for dinner, Max had whispered to Aunt Evie, "I have a concern about Tess, Aunt Evie."

That was how he'd put it which was odd itself but also, it was an unspoken rule—they never complained about each other behind the other one's back.

"She's acting very peculiarly," he'd said. "She's having nightmares. Very very vivid ones," he said. "And, she thinks she has a migraine and she's seeing spots."

If one of them was having a problem, they'd both come and talk to her. Or just have a fight in front of her. They didn't speak behind each other's backs. It seemed to violate the sacred oath of the Pinkie swear. Aunt Evie exhaled. Maybe they *were* just becoming teenage.

"How's your head, Tess?" asked Aunt Evie, when she saw Tess squinting her eyes as she looked across the room.

Tess gave "the person who used to be Max" an evil look, because she hadn't told Aunt Evie that she'd had a headache. "Fine, Aunt Evie," she said cheerfully. "I think I was just hungry and thirsty."

"That's good!" said Aunt Evie. "My friend Bobbie rang up," she said, "asked if I'd run down the road to a pub for a holiday drink." She snortled, which is something short of a laugh but cheerful.

"Is Bobbie a boy or a girl?" asked Tess.

"Girl," said Aunt Evie. "Bestie. But we haven't seen each other for a while. I might be late," she said.

Aunt Evie was definitely looking forward to a couple of hours of grown-up time. And Tess, for one, thought that was great, that Aunt Evie was going out with a friend.

"Have an excellent time," said Tess. "We'll be just fine." But as she said it, Tess realized she had no idea if that was in fact going to be true . . .

trying to pretend that everything is normal

Do you think there's anything on TV?" Tess asked, as she reached for the remote control on the table in the living room of the suite. "I was hoping maybe there'd be an old movie on. I don't want to watch the news. Maybe there's a mini-series on, preferably not a crime one, one with a real story," she said sort of wistfully. "One that Mom might like." Tess hit the remote control "on" button, but nothing happened.

"Do you think there's another remote?" she asked "Max," quite certain he would know the answer, but he stared at her blankly. Then she remembered, "the person who used to be Max" might not be as attuned to electronics as her brother was. She tried screaming at him, "Max!! Max!!" but he just kept staring at her silently.

"This dress is very uncomfortable," she said, quietly, her voice breaking, almost to herself. "I think I'll go and change before I tackle the television. . . ." It was sort of an excuse because she was close to tears and the last thing she wanted was for "the person who used to be Max" to see her cry. She didn't know why but she was certain that wasn't a good idea. Inside her head, she was screaming, "Max?!! Max?!! Are you in there?!"

Black jeans. That was what she wanted to wear. She hung her dress up carefully but didn't realize as she slipped it off over her head that the cat's eye marble dropped out and rolled across the floor.

She pulled her black jeans out of the bottom drawer and put them on. White t-shirt. She wanted to wear a black t-shirt but that was too dark. Black belt. Plain, no buckle to speak of. Black socks and her sort of tennis shoes, also black, that were a little more like ballet shoes, very light with almost no sole, thin laces, so you could walk carefully, almost on a tightrope if one was around, or if you wanted to, trudge through a field. She didn't know that both of them would be needed. But she had a feeling it was going to be a long night.

She had to get Max out of there. Or did she have to get Colin out of there—it was very confusing—without doing any harm to Max. *Why? Why had it happened? The boy must want something.* That was all she could figure out. Colin must want something. She didn't want to believe that he was just evil.

Time was doing that funny thing again. Where a minute felt longer than it was and then a half hour could go by almost in an instant. Time, in Tess's experience, was variable.

She'd never felt so alone before.

strange breaths

It was cold, so cold. It felt like a brisk wind was blowing through the room. Outside in the garden, icicles had formed on the branches of the tree again and they were sparkling in the moonlight. The weather had been so changeable. And it looked as if it might change again.

"The person who used to be Max" had a button-down sweater on, cashmere, for sure. Tess wondered where that was from. But maybe boys borrowed clothes, too. That made sense. Except he was shivering. He was so cold. His lips were practically blue against his pale opaque white skin.

Max wasn't that pale. He'd never been that pale.

He opened his mouth as if to speak to her, but only a puff of air came out. The way one breathes outside on a cold day when your breath is hotter than the air. Except it wasn't quite like an exhaled breath, more like a waft of white smoke that curled up strangely in the air. And then another. And then a funny sound inside his chest, as if he was trying to breathe.

Max sometimes got asthma. But Tess didn't think that this was that.

No one had built a fire in their room that day. Tess didn't see any logs by the hearth or she would have attempted it. She could time his breaths by the wispy white smoke in the air. He seemed to be breathing slowly, so slowly.

Was he trying to tell her something?

There was so much time between each breath.

It felt as if time itself had slowed even more. Tess couldn't tell if there were twenty seconds or longer between each of the breaths, or if you could even call it a breath. There were just wisps of bright white smoke curling up in the air.

Tess realized she had been holding her breath.

People did that sometimes when they were frightened. At least that's what her dad said. And then he'd given them advice, "Breathe. Always remember to breathe. Especially if something's making you anxious."

Tess let her breath out, then breathed in deeply, then let it out again and realized there was no visible sign of *her* breath, no white wisps of smoke when she breathed. Just his. And his breaths were coming at strange irregular intervals.

As she walked towards him, Tess felt as if she was moving in slow motion, too, as if there was resistance in the air and she was moving through a haze or a fog. *Maybe she could reach Max. Maybe if she did something completely Max-like, she could get him to come back.*

"Let's go up to the library," she said. "Please, Max." *Maybe, if she spoke to Max, she could bring him back.* "I'll play chess with you, Max. I don't mind if you win. . . ."

The boy nodded. Tess picked up the key. And put it in her front jeans pocket. "I'll race you," she said.

Tess knew there'd be a real fire burning in the fireplace in the library and "Max" or "the person who used to be Max" was so cold. She grabbed the blanket off his cot and went to race him. She was very relieved when he ran after her, so relieved, she shut the hotel room door and forgot to lock it.

CHAPTER TWENTY-THREE

strange exit

The library wasn't any warmer. No one had built a fire there either. It looked different somehow. There were definitely more books on the shelves, maybe someone had restocked them, and there was a pair of slippers on the carpet in front of the comfortable wingchair upholstered with beige silk fabric dotted with pale pink flowers. Everything seemed to have been fluffed up, an expression her mom would use, the cushions placed just so on the sofa, the mahogany coffee table shiny, with a slight hint of the scent of lemon oil in the room, as if all of the wood had been polished, too, including the bannister that led down to the lobby.

It was cold. So cold. Maybe the heat was out. That must be it. Tess wanted to tell someone at the desk, but she hadn't seen anyone in the lobby when they walked through it. *Strange.*

The chess board was set up. "Sit there," she said. "You always like to play black and give me the white advantage as you should. You're so much better at chess than I am."

The boy nodded at her. *That was how she was going to think of him now. Just as "the boy."* She tried to convince herself that Max was in there somewhere, if she could only reach him. *Max. Max!!* She and Max used to think they had almost psychic communication. But the boy just sat there in the chair where she directed him to sit down.

He was so cold. Tess wrapped the blanket around him. And rubbed his hands, the way their mom would do in New York in the winter sometimes when they'd come home from school. Tess wished she'd brought a blanket for herself. She saw a small, soft gray blanket folded over the arm of the sofa and wrapped that around herself, like a shawl, and sat down across from him.

He was so pale.

She moved her Queen's pawn up. That was the safest move. At least that was what Max had told her.

He picked up his left knight as if he was going to move it but instead he seemed to almost freeze. It reminded her of what Colin had done when Max had played table hockey with him. He sat there frozen in mid-air.

"Max!! Max!!" She couldn't help it. She screamed at him. "Max! Max!" But it was as if he didn't see her.

And then his eyes blinked. She hadn't realized it, but it was almost as if they hadn't blinked before. But it was as if he had been frozen somehow in time. He was still holding the knight tightly in his hand. He got up from the table. He turned away from her. And began to walk away. And Tess watched as he walked right—she had to be imagining it—as she watched him walk straight through the wall . . . and simply disappear.

"Maaaxxx!!"

It was still freezing in the room. But there wasn't a visible crack in the wall. Nothing. Just her. In the empty library with one white Queen's pawn moved up one spot and, as if in punctuation, the other side of the board set up perfectly except that one of the black knights was missing.

"Maaxxx!!"

She ran down the small flight of stairs to the lobby. There was no one there. At least, that what she thought at first. But then she saw the gentleman with the bowler hat, the one who owned Princess, sitting in an armchair in the corner. She ran over to him to beg him to help her. "Please!" she said. He was staring straight ahead as if he didn't even see her and couldn't hear her pleas. She sat down in the chair next to him.

"Please. Please!" she said. "Won't you help. I think my brother's . . ." But before she could finish the sentence, she saw the gentleman's face begin to crack and tiny pieces start to break away, first his cheek and then part of his nose as if he was made of plaster. The wall behind him started to crack as well. And all the papers neatly stacked behind the bell desk flew from their spots and scattered across the room as if a wind was blowing, a lampshade flew sideways.

As if by instinct, Tess reached into her front jeans pocket for the marble but realized it wasn't there. She hadn't put it in her jeans when she'd changed her clothes. Not that she was sure that it would help.

The massive chandelier with the hanging prisms in the lobby began to shake as if it could fall from the ceiling. She looked over at the armchair where the gentleman had been sitting but all that was there was a cloud of dust.

Tess ran from the room towards The Garden Room, only to find that the door was open.

"Maaxx!! Maaxx!!" She called out, hoping he might be there.

But the only thing that answered her was the wind.

the cat's eye marble

Tess ran to the closet in her bedroom, pulled her denim dress off the hanger. But the marble wasn't there—the cat's eye marble wasn't in either of the dress pockets. Maybe she'd put it down. That had to be it. Maybe she'd put it on the bedside table, before she took the dress off. She checked both of them. It wasn't there. She ran back into the living room of the suite in the hope it might be on one of the side tables of the couch. But it wasn't there either. She knelt on the rug and pulled the edge of the couch up to look under it. But it wasn't there either. She had to find it.

She realized it wasn't Max she had to find, it was Colin. Max couldn't walk through a wall. And the only thing she had that linked her to Colin was the cat's eye marble that she believed belonged to him and that she thought had powers of its own. She had to get to the other side of the wall. . . .

Then she remembered looking for the remote control. It was so cold in the room. . . . But she was so upset, she couldn't even feel the cold. She ran over to the table where the TV was and the remotes. But the cat's eye marble wasn't there either.

At least the walls seemed solid in The Garden Room. That was something anyway. The chandelier wasn't swinging. She walked back into the bedroom. Had she gone into the bathroom and she hadn't remembered? Her mom often left her rings on the sink when she washed her hands. *No, there was nothing there either.*

She walked over to the bed, uncertain what to do. She thought about lying down, pretending none of it had happened and she would wake up soon. "Maaxx! Maaxx!" But nothing answered her but the wind.

And then she saw something jostle the skirt of the elaborately made bed. And then tap it again. She wasn't imagining it. And then a paw, an orange paw with white stripes. And then the cat's eye marble came flying across the floor directly to her, followed by Ginger whose paw it was.

Tess leaned down and picked it up immediately and closed her right hand around it. It was warm, not as warm as it usually was. But it was warm. And she bent down to pet the cat and say, "thank you." She deposited the marble safely into her front jeans pocket and without even thinking about what danger might lie ahead, ran back through the lobby to head up the stairs again to the library. It *was* something their Dad always said. "If you get lost, try to get back to where you started, if you can." He always added that part, "if you can."

CHAPTER TWENTY-FIVE

trying to get back to where she started

She ran through the wreck of the lobby. She stared straight ahead as she ran, so as not to be distracted or frightened by any of the chaos or destruction. She had her right hand in her jeans pocket, holding tightly onto the marble, as if it might somehow protect her.

She ran up the short flight of stairs into the library, only to find that the old-fashioned wooden door that she'd never noticed before was closed. She tried the door-knob, but the door appeared to be locked.

She had to get inside. There wasn't any other choice. She had to get back into the library. She tried the knob again, it turned but the door wouldn't budge. It was locked up tight.

Then she remembered, she had the key to The Garden Room in in her left pocket, not that that would work. . . . But it was an elaborate key, with the blown glass prism on top that had the red swirls inside, sort of like the cat's eye marble in her other pocket. *Maybe it was a master key. Maybe.*

Tess took it out of her pocket. She shut her eyes and made a wish and when she opened them, the key was sparkling. Brilliantly sparkling. And then emitting sparks. And, almost as if it was magnetically attracted, drawn to the keyhole where it affixed itself and turned almost by itself. Tess turned the doorknob and was able to open the door to the library.

But it wasn't a library. It was a boy's bedroom—at least she thought it was a boy's. There was a dark plaid bedspread displayed on the old-fashioned brass bed, with matching pillow cases. The chairs were covered in brown corduroy fabric, made slightly more comfortable by navy-blue throw pillows. There was a standing hockey game table in the back of the room that looked a lot like the hockey table Max and Colin had played on in Colin's room only two nights before, although it looked slightly newer. In fact, the room looked a lot like Colin's room. She put the key back in her pocket.

She was holding the marble with her other hand. She let go of it and took that hand out of her pocket, too. But the room stayed the same.

She was in a room that looked like an old-fashioned boy's room. No library. No chess-table. No bar. She looked down the stairs to see if she might have taken a wrong turn but no, she hadn't.

She remembered Adele's words again, "There's something on the other side of the wall."

In the corner, there was a desk, an old-fashioned desk, modest, not too elaborate, as if it was a desk for a kid. There was a paperweight on it, which Tess realized instantly had the same orange blown glass center as the cat's eye marble and similar to the key, as if they were all part of a set or had been made by the same glass blower.

The desk was very tidy but there was a note on it. Tess wondered if that was an ethical dilemma—if you find a note on somebody's desk are you allowed to read it? Was it sort of like looking at somebody's email without their permission? And then she realized it wasn't. Because she didn't know where she was, and if there was a clue there somehow, she had to read it.

The first thing that struck her was the date:

December, 1926
Three Days before Christmas

And then she recognized the stationery. It said at the very top, centered and engraved in black ink:

SANBORN HOUSE

And nothing else. No identifying address underneath. Just *Sanborn House*. It was a note from Colin's mother, handwritten, in an old-fashioned ink-pen-perfect curlicue way.

Dear Colin...

And then his mother went on to tell him in the note that she and his father were going out that night to a party and asked if he would help take care of his sister Lizzie. Not much more than that.

Except that it was December, 1926. That was the date. *Three Days before Christmas.*

Tess reasoned, *hotels like to hold onto history and sometimes display historical items.* But she touched the paper and it was thin, exquisitely thin, but not the least bit fragile. There's a way paper feels when it's new that is very different from the way paper feels when it's old or even been sitting around for a few years. And this had been sitting around for . . . Tess hated to think how long. Or had it? It didn't feel brittle at all. It felt new. She put the letter down and picked up the glass paperweight with the orange swirls inside from the desk. It, too, was warm when she touched it, the way the marble had been.

She looked around the room and now it was different even than the room she'd walked into. At least the way she'd walked in was gone. There was no longer a staircase down to the lobby.

In fact, it didn't seem as if there were any doors, at all. There was a window and outside Tess could see, even though it was nighttime, the snow falling again. White snow, sparkling against the street lamps.

Tess held on to the paperweight more tightly.

It was so strange to be in a room where there weren't any doors, at all.

Still holding on to the paperweight in her right hand, as if by instinct, with her left hand, she pulled the cat's eye marble from her pocket and held it up, too. Instantly, there were orange vectors of light beaming perfectly like straight lines at different angles from both the center of the paperweight and the interior of the marble, pointing directly towards the wall.

The wall that "the person who used to be Max" had walked through. At least the same wall that "the person who used to be Max" had walked through when the room was a library . . .

The cat's eye marble was blasting out bright orange, almost like neon colored lights, straight lines at angles which were emanating from the center of the blown glass marble directly towards the wall. It was a bit like a laser show, or something that might be given off from a small rocket as it was taking off, or the tail of a comet in space. The marble was hot to the touch and so was the paperweight and actually Tess worried one of them might liquify in her hand.

But the vectors of orange light just kept streaming towards the wall. And then they stopped. Just like that. As if each of the objects had run out of fuel. Or worn themselves out.

She set the paperweight back on the desk. She looked down at the marble. No, it was the same. It hadn't changed. The cat's eye marble was still intact in her hand as was the paperweight, inert, innocent as if neither object had done anything, at all.

Except there was an open doorway. Just that. An open doorway. Tess couldn't even tell if there was a door. Just an open doorway that led to a dark unknown hallway beyond.

Adele was standing there now, tiny, knowing, standing quietly by the open doorway. "You can't stay here," she said. "You know that. You have to go find Colin."

And as she said it, Tess looked around the room and knew that was probably true. She didn't know where she was. The only way out seemed the open doorway that would lead her to she had no idea where. And something else resonated for her. Adele had said, she had to go find Colin. Was it Colin she was trying to reach, not Max? Or that the only way she could reach Max was by finding Colin and communicating with him? She would have to get over being angry at Colin, if that was going to work, have a civil discourse with him. But maybe she could get him to apologize first. If she could find him. If only, she could find him and find Max . . . or "the person who used to be Max" and try, if she could turn him into Max again. . . .

She looked around the room. She had no idea if she'd taken a step back in time or if time had shifted, or it was just a dream she might not wake up from, but the only way out seemed to be the strange open doorway that had somehow presented itself in the wall and that was probably the only way to find Colin or as she now called him, "the person who used to be Max."

Tess looked back at the strange doorway, as if to study it—the strange doorway where only a moment ago, Adele had been standing—and realized she was all alone in the room now. Adele had vanished, too. And the room was getting darker by the moment, as if all light and air was being pulled from it as she stood there.

She held the marble in her hand and ran through the open doorway stepping into an absence of light, a kind of darkness that was stranger than any she'd ever encountered before. . . .

CHAPTER TWENTY-SIX

1926: three days before christmas

December, 1926
Three Days before Christmas

At least that was the date on the note his mother had left on his desk in her ink pen-perfect-curlicue-handwriting.

Anyone else might have written the 22nd of December. But his mother loved holidays, so to her it was "Three Days before Christmas." The exquisite floral and pine cone wreath, dotted with red berries, lavender, and thyme had been hanging on the front door since the first day of December. The tree had been decorated weeks ago. The large mercury ornaments in the shape of stars and globes, silvery and reflective, were so heavy they had to be tied to the branches with string that was dyed green to match the tree. The crystal glass ornaments, balls, and prisms were so fragile that only she was allowed to hang them, very carefully with thick silver thread, real silver. The garlands were made from fresh holly.

Colin and Elizabeth, his younger sister, had a few ornaments of their own. He had a wood block with a C on it with a picture of a cat and a clown—both "C" words. She had one with an E with a picture of an elephant and an egg. Colin had three small painted ceramic elves that his mother said were from Scotland. But Colin thought most elves lived in Ireland, so he wasn't sure she was right. His sister had a tiny metal fire engine that had a bell that occasionally rang when no one was expecting it, which their mother thought was funny, too. There were wooden soldiers, actually miniatures of the guards at Buckingham Palace, in red coats fastened with tiny gold buttons. It was always such a nice day when the boxes with the ornaments appeared in the living room and they knew the Christmas tree would be arriving (as if by magic) shortly.

Anyway, it was three days before Christmas and his mother had left him a note on his desk:

SANBORN HOUSE

December, 1926
Three Days before Christmas

Dear Colin,
Your father and I are going to a party.
Hannah has made dinner for you and Lizzie.
Swedish meatballs. Your favorite. We might be
late. You know how the Bennetts like to celebrate
holidays. Tree trimming. Carolers. I hear there
may be a five-piece quartet (I guess that would
be a quintet) and a choir. And probably sticky
toffee pudding. For sure, I'll bring you both
chocolates, I promise.
Please see that Lizzie doesn't stay up too late.
And if you would, would you read her a book?
Extra Kisses,
Mama

Colin had done exactly what his mother had wished. He'd even read a chapter of *Doctor Dolittle's Caravan* to Lizzie after she'd put on her pajamas and hopped into bed. Lizzie was eight and they'd had a long day and she fell asleep as he was reading to her. She looked so peaceful. He tucked the covers gently under her chin and stroked the top of her head, the way his mother did to him sometimes, before he went off to school. He put the book back on the shelf, turned the lamp off by her bed, and walked quietly out of the room so as not to wake her.

He went to his room and lay down on his bed meaning to read a bit himself, and without meaning to fell asleep.

There was a light snow falling. He wasn't sure what had awakened him but when he woke up he saw the snow and that was what had caused him to go outside. He'd never seen snow falling before.

It hardly ever snowed in London. He'd seen snow on the ground before.

His dad had taken him once to Dartmoor, in South Devon but inland and very high up from the sea, to a friend's manor house that looked more like a castle, and there was snow knee-deep on the ground, soft, lovely for playing in. There'd been a random snowball fight started by a couple of kids on the moor and even his dad had joined in. Gentle throwing, so no one would get hurt. But they'd all ended laughing and rolling in the snow.

It was the snowfall that caused him to go outside. He'd put on his clothes and walked quietly past Lizzie's room and, carrying his boots, tiptoed three flights down the staircase to the front door. It wasn't until he was outside that he sat on the stoop to put his boots on.

He was mesmerized by the snow. He thought it was the most beautiful thing he'd ever seen as it reflected on the street lamps, causing a spray of colors in the air.

Rather than just stand by the streetlight or twirl around, his arms outspread in the falling snow, something compelled him to start to walk to the park.

Snowflakes were falling all around him, like soft petals. And he imagined them sparkling on his cheeks when they landed. But it was so far to walk. And he could feel that his cheeks were rosy from the cold and possibly the tip of his nose was turning red.

A carriage stopped for him. The driver from next door, who was on his way home, and offered him a ride.

Colin hopped up into the seat next to the driver, who smiled at him and said, "And where did you think you'd want to go, my boy?"

"Hyde Park, of course," Colin answered.

There was a Christmas festival in Hyde Park. His mother had told him she'd already seen it set up. They'd gone last year. Not that he thought the rides would be running at midnight or the Ferris wheel, especially given the snowstorm, but nonetheless, the park seemed like a large expanse, a brilliant canvas on which to see a blanket of white powdery snow that had already covered the ground. A place where there might be a way to make snowballs and maybe a sculpture of a castle.

When they arrived at Hyde Park, there was snow on the ground, lots of it. The kind gentleman let him off at the corner. The snow was sparkly, at first, lit by the street lamps.

He hadn't counted on how dark it was going to be when he entered and started to wade through the snow, deeper and deeper into the park . . .

CHAPTER TWENTY-SEVEN

the other side of the wall

Tess had a feeling she was in a hallway, even though she couldn't feel a wall on either side of her. Was the ground beneath her feet solid? Was there ground beneath her feet? Or could she just step forward and there wouldn't be ground, walk off at any moment if the ground stopped and fall into the giant void of nothingness. There was darkness all around her.

She held the marble up as if it could somehow be

a guiding light. But still there was only darkness. A strange kind of darkness as if she was in a cave or tunnel or a hallway except that there weren't any walls.

She held the marble still, flat now in her palm, and held it up, almost at an angle as if it could show the way, and suddenly the passageway lit up. Well, sort of lit up. There were all kinds of turns and angles. They were lit, the turns and the angles, bright orange, but the passageway itself was still pretty dark. There were strange reflections of light in the darkness, straight geometric lines at all kinds of angles and levels, vectors of orange neon light, very much like the ones she'd seen in her dream.

Was she supposed to duck or walk over them? Were they like a warning system that could go off at any minute, sirens would sound, or the walls would collapse? She was letting her imagination run away with itself. Was she really? There were vectors of light everywhere she turned, and she had gone through a doorway that hadn't been there before and seemed, when she looked back, to have closed behind her. Not only closed. The wall itself appeared to have closed up, realigned itself, and there wasn't even a door any more or a doorway to run back through. Tess didn't want to think about what she would do if she couldn't get back. Or couldn't find "the person who used to be Max," or was it Colin, who'd gone through the library wall.

And now, she had, too. She knew she was on the other side of the wall or maybe even more peculiarly inside of the wall, in a tunnel of some sort or a hallway that led she wasn't sure where.

At least, she could see there *were* walls at the moment, even though they veered in strange angles and directions, including up and down.

Her instinct was, if she hit a corner and had to make a choice, it made more sense to go down. At least that would make sense if she believed the message that Colin had scrawled on the bottom of his mother's note.

Dear Mums & Papa,

I woke up and the most amazing thing happened—I've never seen it snow before, not falling snow, anyway. I didn't want you to worry, if you come home before me.

Don't be mad. I couldn't help it. I had to go out for a moment and watch. I took mittens and boots and my overcoat and will tiptoe so as not to wake Lizzie. I put a note under Hannah's door, so she knows to get

Lizzie if she has one of her funny dreams
and wakes up before I get back.... Don't be
mad. It was so pretty and I think I just have
the holiday spirit.

Hugs,
Colin

Tess looked down and tried to figure out what course to take, how she could navigate the orange vectors. She knew it was probably not a good idea to run into any of them. At the moment, she was trying to delicately balance on one of them, as she'd stepped directly on it when she first went through the wall. If she were to slip, would she fall or get stopped, rather unpleasantly, she imagined, by one of them.

She wondered *if* she could walk with certainty or if there was a possibility she might fall through one of them. *How stable were they? Would she be able to keep her balance? What would happen if she did fall?* She could imagine Max suggesting, as the vectors sometimes crisscrossed at funny angles, that she try not to run into one of them; if she was on one and another one popped up in front of her, that it probably wasn't a good idea to interfere with their space. Or that they might be like a spider web, interwoven somehow, and if one of them were to break, it might be the same as a large glass window shattering. *Max would think that way. As if they might have an attitude or a design of their own.* They probably were there for a reason, whatever the reason was. And they were bright orange, almost like a warning sign and definitely had a maze-like quality, that she thought she should try to figure out before she attempted a run on them. Max had taught her to be a little more careful. Max would say, for sure, that she should study them before she attempted a run on them. At least that was what she thought Max would say if he was with her. She wished he *was* with her to tell her what he really thought.

But he wasn't.

Max was somewhere out there with Colin on the other side of the wall. *Or was he?*

She saw something crouching below her on one of the orange vectors, hunched up against the wall, as if he was hiding in the corner (or waiting for her). It was "the person who used to be Max." He put his index finger up to his mouth as if to say "Shhhh!" Then covered his mouth with his hand, as if imploring her to stay quiet. His finger up again, "Shhh!" as his eyes begged her not to say a word. Tess understood the meaning, that somehow she wasn't supposed to speak, as if the sound of her voice, any sound could set off an alarm, disturb the vectors—she wasn't sure what—but the eyes that were looking at her, imploring her to silence, looked like Max's. "The person who used to be Max" looked like Max again.

Tess put her index finger up to her own mouth, in a gesture of "Shh," and nodded that she understood.

And then the boy's eyes went vacant again, as if there was nobody there.

But that wasn't entirely true either as a moment later, he stood up. All she could see was the back of him. He was balancing himself, one foot in front of the other on one of the orange vectors. He put his arms out, sort of the way you put your arms out if you're gliding or trying to keep your balance on a skateboard or a snowboard, bent his knees down in sort of the same way you might try to glide down a snowy mountainside or the mouth or bowl at a skateboard park. Every time he put one foot in front of another, he seemed to almost slide. He looked back at her for a moment, his eyes still vacant, that slight "Colin" smile on his face, as if he was enticing her and at the same time, trying to demonstrate how she might do it, navigate her way down behind him. He was quite a bit ahead going down a straight vector that was angled toward the—she didn't know if it was ground or what might be at the bottom of the other side of the wall. . . .

Tess ducked beneath one of the orange vertical lines, then she popped up just past it, and kept on sliding, one foot in front of the other, the way he'd shown her. That worked. She jumped over one. That worked, too, landing efficiently at a dead stop on another orange vector. But then it got complicated and Tess could see that some of the vectors of light crossed each other. Which direction was she supposed to go?

It reminded her of the tightrope at the carnival last summer and her friends, the twins, the amazing aerial ballet stars. She'd been able to handle that. Although supposedly there'd been a net below her then.

This time, there was just vast, dark emptiness below, as if she *could* fall into a void and never be heard of again or fall flat onto a surface, so far down it wasn't even visible, and no one would ever know.

But "the person who used to be Max" was efficiently gliding below her and she knew that she had to follow him, figure out a course that she could take.

She swerved to the right, bravely placing her right foot on another orange vector of light, just below her, that ran like a straight line down, her toe balanced at first, and then all her weight on her right foot, and then her left foot after it. Her arms out in the air for balance as he'd shown her. Then launched into a slide.

Don't think about it. Just navigate as if you're on a solid substance through the air. Don't think about how thin it is or if you could fall. Just walk, glide, pretend you're on a skateboard, if you had to put one foot in front of the other, keep balancing with your hands if you must, and holding yourself high, perfect posture, like a ballerina running across a stage. Or if you need to, crouch down for a moment to get up to speed.

The orange vector became like a runway for her, as if she was a model stepping downstairs, except it was flat and slanted and kind of like a skatepark or a perfectly powdered mountain slope.

She looked down at herself, not below, trying not to look below, and was surprised she was wearing what appeared to be a flowy skirt, cut like ribbons, so she could actually dance, and white satin ballet shoes that were tied in perfect crosses up her leg, almost like toe shoes, except they were soft, malleable, so she could actually slide, point one foot up and down in front of her and glide, her arms now out almost floating in the air for balance in a perfect ballerina pose. She had to be imagining it. And then there was light above her, like a spotlight or was it a skylight? She could see the moon above brilliantly outlined against a stream of perfectly white falling snow.

The vector ended and, hesitatingly, she stepped, as there wasn't any other choice, onto what felt like a wood floor. She looked down at her feet and there were her favorite sneakers, the ones that were a bit like ballet shoes themselves. And her black jeans. In front of her was a doorway that looked oddly familiar, strangely like the doorway to the hotel. She could see through the windows on either side that there was snow falling and collecting on the ground. She pulled the door open and ran outside, down the steps, and on to the sidewalk. And she looked to the right, down the street, nothing. But when she looked to the left, she saw a boy from the back whose image looked a lot like Max, walking down the street with his arms outstretched, and watched as a carriage stopped for him and after a moment, he stepped up to the front of the carriage next to the driver.

"No, wait, Maxxx!" she screamed out to him.

And the only answer was the snow falling softly down around her and the distant hoofbeats and wheels turning on cobblestones as the carriage sped briskly away down the London street.

The street itself looked different. Across the street there were only houses. Tess was sure across the street there'd been another hotel. A little bigger than theirs. She remembered its name. It was called *The Splendid*, and she and Aunt Evie had discussed going there one day for tea when her mother arrived. A girls' day. But right now, there were only houses. And a few cars. They didn't look the least bit modern. And she could hear the distant sound of hoofbeats as "the person who used to be Max" seemed to be riding away in the carriage.

Suddenly she felt a hand on her elbow. She looked up to see Mr. Cortland. "I was wondering when you were going to find your way out," he said. "We have to hurry."

He lifted Tess into the front seat next to him in his carriage that was parked at the curb. "Go on, Comet. Go on," he said to the horse, impatiently clicking his tongue the way he had, except he was also brandishing a tiny whip, which he gave the horse a sharp tap with, and expertly handled the reins to turn the horse and the carriage around. "Faster, Comet. Faster. Run like you're dancing in the sky."

Tess held onto the seat as Comet was racing so quickly the carriage itself was almost rocking from side to side. And then—Tess swore that this was true—it was as if Comet was able to, levitate would be the right word, or simply fly just off the ground, carrying the carriage behind her through mid-air, cold air, spectacularly dotted with snow which was falling like petals all around them.

They could barely see through the snow. Mr. Cortland leaned over to Tess and echoed what he'd said when they'd first met. "Don't worry about Comet. She knows the way."

The way to where, Tess wondered. She could no longer see in front of her the carriage that "the person who used to be Max" had stepped in to. There was just a blanket of snow all around them.

"Don't worry. She's got a nose on her," he said reassuringly. "Don't you Comet?"

Comet shook her mane as if she was answering. And took a right turn in the sky without even being led to. As below her, off in the distance, Tess could see what she thought was the carriage that was ferrying "the person who used to be Max" to wherever he was going. At least she hoped that was the carriage she could see below her in the distance . . .

• • •

Tess wasn't surprised when they landed, lightly, as if they'd never been flying, at all, and pulled up to Hyde Park, and

Mr. Cortland brought the carriage to a stop at the corner. It was as if Comet had known where they were going. *A perfect place to see the snow.* Except that there was so much snow now, it was hard to make out anything else. She could see the Ferris wheel up high in the background, stationary, with snow falling all around it.

Tess thought it was the carriage they'd been following parked right in front of them, the one that she'd seen "the person who used to be Max" step in to. But the driver pulled the reins and turned the carriage around and drove right past them. He passed so closely that Tess could see that only the driver was in the front seat and there was no one sitting in the carriage.

Tess jumped down without waiting for Mr. Cortland to come around the side. She could see footprints and a path straight through the snow in the park, as if someone had recently walked there and left a path behind them. The snow was so high—she reasoned it was almost up to her shoulder now—with no sign of the snowfall stopping. And no sign of "the person who used to be Max," just the trace of footsteps deep in the snow going into the park and she reasoned that must have been where he went except she couldn't catch any sight of him.

CHAPTER TWENTY-EIGHT

venturing into the park

Mr. Cortland jumped down from the driver's seat and quick as a wink unbridled Comet, freeing her from the carriage.

He led Comet over to Tess, gently holding onto the reins as he guided her. The horse was unsaddled but there was a blanket across her back obviously intended to help the beloved horse stay warm.

Comet's eyes were clear and knowing and she looked directly at Tess as Mr. Cortland, with a nod, handed the reins over.

Tess realized she didn't have a moment to consider it. There was not time to make any other choice. She put her foot in Mr. Cortland's outstretched cupped hand, as a way to lift her on to the back of Comet as Tess threw her right leg over the horse's back, and took her seat, holding the reins firmly in her hand.

"It's all right," Tess whispered to Comet. "I know that we can find them." She used the word "them" on purpose. Tess knew that she had to find Colin in order to find Max. Or maybe it was the other way around. But it was both of them she had to find.

She remembered Adele's words about Colin, "You're the only who can put him back on solid ground." And while Tess didn't exactly know what that meant, she was certain that moment was starting now. She was starting to understand why Colin might have done this. And the anger she felt at him was starting to melt even though the snow was still falling all around her.

"Don't worry Tess. Don't worry about Comet," said Mr. Cortland. "She knows the way. And, from what I've heard about you, you do, too.

"Take care of her," he added. It wasn't clear whether it was Tess or Comet he was speaking to.

"Ready?" he asked Tess.

She nodded and remembering her manners, she said quietly, almost mouthing the words, "Thank you. I promise," she said as if she was making a sacred vow, "I'll see you again."

There was no time to waste. There was no sight of "the person who used to be Max." And Mr. Cortland made that funny noise he made with his tongue, as if he was clicking it against his cheek, and Comet took off, with full credit to her name, like a rocket through the snowy plough, along the path that Tess could only hope had been made by "the person who used to be Max."

It wasn't a question of holding on—there was no saddle, no stirrups, simply the reins—it was more as if she was truly one with the horse, her body completely in tune with Comet, her legs tightly latched to the horse's sides, leaning in, completely in step and in tune with Comet's rhythmic canter and their steady quest for "the person who used to be Max."

The snow was all around them, high like a wall or a patch in-between two sides of a mountain, as they raced along the slim visible trail like it was a championship Olympic event and they were on a competitive sled ride. Except the only thing they were racing was time, as the snow continued to build up around them, filling in the path, and the only way forward was by instinct.

"Don't worry about Comet," Mr. Cortland had said. "She knows the way."

The way where? Tess wondered. And she couldn't help wondering if she also knew the way back.

The snow seemed to stop at a moment, strangely. As if they'd hit the end of the road.

Comet stopped abruptly, and Tess had to hold herself from tumbling forward as the horse came to a dead stop.

"Colin!!" She knew it was Colin, now. She could tell even from the back. She could see him standing in front of her. He stood straighter than Max did, slightly taller, although oddly more fragile, his arms longer, his presence quieter even as he stood. The snow was still falling. She wondered if he could see that the road had ended. In front of them was a lake, frosted over as if it had iced.

And she watched as he stepped onto the icy surface and, in less than a step forward, fell into the freezing water below.

"Max!!" she screamed and immediately screamed again, "Colin!!" hoping one of them could hear her.

She could only imagine how cold it must be and see that he might never be able to find a way out of the lake, as the surface was completely frosted over.

There wasn't a moment to think about what she

could do. Tess jumped from her mount and dove, directly down into the freezing cold water that startled her through to inside of her bones, as if cold mercury was running through her veins, and her lungs were in danger of collapsing. She held her breath and dove, deep down until she found him.

She and Max used to have psychic communication. "Max!!!" she screamed in her mind. And embraced him with both of her arms. And then she did the same thing to Colin, hoping he might be able to hear her, too. Holding her breath underwater, "Colin!!" she screamed in her mind, as she held onto him tighter.

He didn't fight her. He didn't have much fight in him at that point. It was as if he was frozen through. She didn't let herself think about whether he was breathing. She kicked as hard as she could, kicked them up to the surface. And swam to the edge and managed to push all of them onto the snow.

"Max!!"

But nobody answered.

"Colin!"

Nobody answered again.

"Max!!" She started to pound softly on his chest. And took a deep breath and breathed into him. She pounded again on his chest and took another deep breath and breathed it into him.

And he sputtered. She'd never been so happy to hear such a sound. He sputtered and coughed. She lifted him slightly and hit him harder on the back until she was sure, quite certain he was breathing on his own.

She took the blanket from the back of Comet and wrapped herself and him in it. She was as cold as he was. Her fingers were almost blue.

She dropped the blanket for a moment. She held her hand out for Max, cupped it the way Mr. Cortland had but Max (or was it Colin) didn't respond. She picked his foot up and put it into her cupped hand and lifted him onto Comet's back. She pulled the blanket up and rested it in front of him. And then, as there was no stirrup to hold on to, hoisted herself up, one hand on the blanket, as if it was almost the beginning of a somersault for life, and took her place on Comet's back in front of "the person who used to be Max."

She took his hands—they were so cold—and wrapped them around her waist. She pulled the blanket up and tried to wrap it around them. She grabbed the reins. She made that noise, that funny noise that Mr. Cortland made with his tongue, and as if the horse knew exactly where she was going, Comet turned around and started to race back again.

The wind was blowing against them now, or rather the horse was running against the wind which was strong, brisk, and racing as fast as Comet was, as if it was trying to push them back, back into the water. The snowfall was fierce, as well, and furious, as if it was coming down in sheets. It was so cold. It felt like there were tentacles of ice wrapping around them. Tess looked down and thought she saw creatures rising up from the snow like an arctic boa constrictor that had somehow been matched with an octopus, with icy coils for arms that were trying to wrap them and weaving their way up Comet's legs. Tess watched as the arms tried to wrap them and squeeze them, as if they were trying to get them to breathe the very air out of them, squeezing harder even, as if they were trying to get them to shoot up to space.

Tess made that noise again, that clicking noise that Mr. Cortland made with his tongue, and kicked Comet gently with her heels. Comet ran faster still, running past the reach of the first creatures whose arms were like tentacles of ice, racing faster and faster still. And finally, so fast that her pace alone out-distanced the cold and Tess felt the warmth of Comet safely guiding them on.

She stroked the horse's mane and whispered in her ear. "Thank you." And then she said to Max, even though she didn't know if he could hear her, "Hold onto me, please. Hold onto me." She wasn't sure, but she thought she felt his arms tighten around her.

She could hear Mr. Cortland saying again, *Don't worry, she knows the way.* And Tess certainly hoped that was true, as the path they'd travelled had now been covered again by snow and all that was around them was a blanket of white accompanied by the fierce wind and an occasional strange icicle which seemed to be wanting to trap them and pull them back towards the lake.

Tess touched her hair and wasn't surprised that it felt stiff, almost as if it was frozen. Of course, it did, she'd been in the water. She'd rescued "the person who used to be Max" who was now holding on to her. She wanted to turn back and see him, but Comet was racing so quickly that she didn't have the chance. She had to lean in and race with the horse as if they were one and hold onto the belief that what she felt was Max's arms around her.

Still holding on to the reins with one hand, Tess reached back and put her arm around "Max's" waist. He was so cold that she felt a shiver run through her, the moment she touched him. But he was there. There, behind her.

"Hold onto me, Max. Hold onto me."

But all that answered her was the wind.

flashback/
flash forward

T ess could see in front of her that the slopes of snow
ended in a moment and they would be out on the street.
Out of the park. Almost on solid ground.

Comet raced on and Tess could hear the almost
metallic sound as her hoofbeat hit the pavement and
Hyde Park was behind them.

The snow wasn't piled up on the street the way it
had been in the park. There was just a fine layer of

snow on the sidewalk and snowflakes gently falling. Tess felt almost as if she'd stepped out of the wake of an avalanche onto solid ground, or come down a mountain to dryer land, or somehow passed through another doorway.

The carriage wasn't parked at the curb. Mr. Cortland was nowhere to be seen. Nor was anyone else. It was the dead of night and only the street lamps were there as their witness.

"The person who used to be Max" was shivering behind her. She turned and saw that his eyes were closed. He was so pale. He was astonishingly pale. And his eyes were closed. There was something about the way his eyes were closed that frightened her.

"Max!! Max!! Wake up!!" And then she had to do something she'd had to do to him once before.

"I'm sorry, Max. I'm sorry," she said—and then she slapped him full-on on the cheek, leaving a red mark where her hand had been. "Wake up, Max!! Wake up!!"

His eyes fluttered but then they shut again. "Hold on to me, Max. Hold on to me. Rest your head on the back of my shoulder."

She felt him do what she had directed. She felt the weight of his head rest against her right shoulder and his hands tighten their grasp around her waist. "Hold on to me, Max. Hold on to me."

There was still no sight of the carriage or of Mr. Cortland.

Her mind was racing. *Why would Colin have done something so evil, stepped into the freezing pond with Max. But then she realized that might not have been what had happened....* Although she wasn't sure what she was imagining could even be true.

The few automobiles visible parked on the street were strangely old-fashioned. The street lamps looked different. London is full of cameras posted on traffic lights but she didn't see any as they sped by, not that she'd noticed any traffic lights either. The few lights visible from inside the houses were dim, muted, and often flickering as if some of them were candlelit. But she reasoned, it was late, and probably a lot of people had gone to sleep. She let her hands go slack on the reins and Comet took it as a sign and slowed down almost to a walk.

Tess leaned in and stroked the horse's mane. It was cold and stiff and dusted with ice. She tried for a moment to untangle it.

She whispered into Comet's ear, "You know the way. My hands are on the reins in case you need me. I know you know the way home."

She remembered what Adele had said, "You're the only one who can put him back on solid ground." Is that what she'd just done or was trying to do now?

Tess made the clicking sound the same way Mr. Cortland had and without a hint of Tess pulling the reins in one direction or another, Comet turned to the left and began, at a trot at first, and then faster, speeding them along the oddly dimly lit London cobblestoned streets.

Tess hadn't remembered that all the streets had been cobblestoned when they went out with Aunt Evie. Maybe it was just that there were cobblestones by the park. Part of London had cobblestones, like the outdoor market at Covent Garden. But Tess remembered the distinct sound from earlier that night, as if all the streets were cobblestoned, and Comet's hoofbeats made their own syncopated rhythm, faster and faster still, against the cobblestoned street.

Comet made another left turn again so quickly that they were in danger of falling off. Tess righted both of them. "Hold on to me!! Hold on."

Comet continued to race so swiftly that it was somewhere beyond a canter. Then Comet made another left turn.

At which point the street looked vaguely familiar. *Had she seen these houses before?*

Up ahead, a crowd had gathered in front of a house.

They were standing almost in a circle, bundled up against the cold, with scarves hastily tied around their necks and heavy overcoats that nobody had stopped to button.

Comet came to a stop. Tess looked over at the people. "What's happened?" she asked. "What's happened?"

But nobody seemed to hear her.

She could see Colin's mother who held the note in her hand. Someone had something like a flashlight and was beaming it on to the note. Someone else was holding what looked like a map as if they were trying to ascertain a possible route. The snow was falling.

Comet hit the pavement with her right foot, forcefully, as if to make a point, causing what looked like a search party to look at her. As everyone looked worried and frantic and about to go out on a hunt in all different directions.

But the expressions on the faces of the people visibly changed from concern to one of joy and amazement as they saw the amazing horse Comet come to a stop at the curb.

And then she heard him whisper in her ear, softly but clear as a bell, the English accent so distinct, "Thank you."

Tess saw the expression on Colin's mother's face as Tess heard someone's feet land on the sidewalk and watched as Colin jumped down from the horse and ran into his mother's arms.

It was a strange sight indeed. The white horse pulling up at the curb with the boy clinging on to the blanket. No one in the search party could see Tess or Max—just a boy named Colin who'd been brought home from his adventure in the snow.

He ran into his mother's arms and there were tears streaming down her cheeks, tears of joy. They were joined in a moment by what looked like Colin's father. The three of them held each other in an embrace. Colin was shivering. His father slid his coat off and placed it around Colin and picked him up in his arms. And Tess watched as the three of them, followed by some of the search party, climbed the steps back to the house, and opened the door to go in. Tess could just get a glimpse of a very large Christmas tree, lovingly and perfectly decorated with silver and glass ornaments and garlands made out of holly, before the front door shut again.

Tess had a moment where she couldn't help but wonder as the door shut behind Colin, if that was what England was always going to be for her, a place where she would meet someone who she might never see again.

And then she felt Max's arms around her waist.

She turned to see him, funny as ever, his glasses halfway down his nose. "Max! Max!!" she called out so happily.

She touched his hair, partly to push the cold ice from it. This time, he didn't flinch, he smiled as she tousled his hair.

"Tess! Tess . . ." he said to her. She'd recognize his voice anywhere, that voice that cracked sometimes as it was becoming deeper. "Where are we, Tess? What's happened to us? I'm so cold. . . . And I appear to be riding on a horse," said Max stating the obvious which was so like Max, Tess started laughing.

Mr. Cortland appeared, hopping down from the seat of his carriage which was still on the corner waiting for them, stationary, permanently in place, with no horse gently bridled in front of it to lead its way. He stroked Comet's mane, then lifted Max down. *It was Max.* Tess knew that it was him. *Just him.* And then he lifted Tess down onto the sidewalk. Without any prompting, Max held his right hand up as did Tess and they executed a pinkie swear in front of what now looked exactly like THE SANBORN HOUSE, complete with a sign, the boutique hotel that she and Max were staying at with Aunt Evie. It was a genuine pinkie swear that indicated that they proudly always had each other's backs, as a taxi pulled up at the curb.

Strange, as it was the middle of the night. Probably somebody who'd been out partying. In a flash, the back door opened, and their mother stepped out of the cab onto the sidewalk, followed by their dad, and they all embraced, laughing.

Their mother didn't say a word of admonishment. She just laughed and said, "I wonder how you knew we were coming?! Did Aunt Evie tell you? We wanted it to be a surprise."

At which point the front passenger door of the cab opened and Aunt Evie stepped out (as she hadn't really gone to a pub to meet a friend, she'd gone to meet their parents at the airport). "I did not say a word to them. I promise," said Aunt Evie.

Their dad looked at them quizzically, taking in the whole scene—Max wrapped in a blanket, Mr. Cortland next to them, as if he was somehow guarding them, the white horse looking as if she had just had the run of her life, and Tess, her hair blown, her cheeks as rosy as if she herself had run a marathon, brave and defiant, as always, smiling so happily, except her lips were a little blue—and because he knew them so well, he said, "And I wonder what you *are* doing up so late at night?"

Tess reached her hand into her pocket. She wrapped her hand tightly on the cat's eye marble. The marble was warm to her touch and then warmer still. And suddenly a faint orange glow seemed to encircle all of them, as if there was a spotlight from the sky onto the sidewalk. And the five of them hugged, as the snow fell softly, like light petals all around them.

thank you

Tess and Max would like to thank the amazing Jill Santopolo for presenting our continuing real and imagined adventures, and Jennifer Chung, Jennifer Bricking, and Vartan Ter-Avanesyan for picturing us and our travels in England; the many magical voices of our friend Laraine Newman; and all the kind people behind the curtain at Philomel Books and Penguin Random House: Ken Wright, the patient and attentive Talia Benamy, Lindsay Boggs, Diane McKiernan, Katherine Punia, and Felicia Frazier!

And all the people who supported Amy: friends and family, Alan Rader, John Byers, Judianna Makovsky, Holly Palance, Sally Singer, Allison Thomas, Wendy Goldberg, Cathryn Michon & Bruce Cameron, Alexandria Jackson, Maia, Matt, Anna, Kevin, and Ethan, Delia, Nick, the inspirational Sonneborn family, Alison Petrocelli, ditto the Morgan family, Nancy Ellison & William Rollnick, the stellar Bob Myman and Jennifer Grega, Scott Miller and Alex Slater, Jon Huddle and Kara Corwin (who know a bit about the strangeness of elevators, too), resident psychic Lila, and a special thanks to Richard Symons, imbedded researcher on Ms. Ephron's ghost travels years ago to England, and his generous participation in, as he states, that "off-road trek across mud-filled fields and into ancient burial sites" in his Aston Martin DB6 which was probably not meant for off-roading in the remote and mystical English countrysides but which is probably where Amy found us!